MURDER AT MIDNIGHT

MARSHALL COOK

TYRUS
BOOKS

Published in electronic format by
TYRUS BOOKS
an imprint of F+W Media, Inc.
10151 Carver Road
Blue Ash, Ohio 45242
www.tyrusbooks.com

eISBN 10: 1-4405-3227-3
eISBN 13: 978-1-4405-3227-6

POD ISBN 10: 1-4405-5390-4
POD ISBN 13: 978-1-4405-5390-5

This is a work of fiction. Names, characters, corporations, institutions, organizations, events,
or locales in this novel are either the product of the author's imagination or, if real, used
fictitiously. The resemblance of any character to actual persons (living or dead) is entirely
coincidental.

This work has been previously published in print format by:
Bleak House Books, Inc.
Print ISBN: 0-9325-5706-7

MURDER AT MIDNIGHT

MARSHALL COOK

PROLOGUE

A long black sedan glides slowly into the parking lot. Its headlights briefly illuminate the statue of the Virgin Mary, then swing to discover the low brick school. The car stops a few feet from the church. The passenger side door opens, releasing a small pool of light and spilling Debussy's *La Mer* into the warm night air. A small man wearing black shirt and slacks and the white clerical collar of the priesthood emerges.

"Are you sure you won't come in for a nightcap?" the small man says, bending down into the still-open doorway.

A thickset man, also yoked with the collar of the priesthood, leans over. "It's late, Michael," he says, "and I have miles to go before I sleep."

"And promises to keep, I'm sure." The little man straightens up, gives his shirt an unnecessary tug, and closes the car door with a solid thump. "Good night, then," he says.

The sedan pulls slowly away. The small priest stands, his right hand in the air, as if blessing the departing man.

The car bellies through the gully and turns onto the highway. The priest slowly mounts the steps of the church, his black wingtips clicking on the concrete. He pauses to peer up into the serene face of the blessed mother. The church behind her is dark, the tall cross on the spire thrusting toward the distant, unblinking stars.

"Hail Mary, full of grace," he murmurs, his voice thick with the brogue he has never lost, "the Lord is with thee. Blessed art thou amongst women, and blessed is the fruit of thy womb, Jesus."

A breeze stirs the leaves in the oaks looming over the church.

He puts a hand on the pedestal, pats it. "Sweet mother of mercy," he says. "Pray for us, that we may be made worthy of the promises of Christ."

He walks the few steps to the church, grasps the handles of the heavy wooden double doors and pulls. The doors stay fast. He shuffles around the far side of the church, where the little cemetery stretches down a gentle slope to the highway. The graves nearest the church run parallel with the highway. He has buried many of their occupants: Schumakers, Grossmans, Kroegers, Voghts, Schmidts. Beyond these, running perpendicular to the highway, a smaller number of tombstones announce the resting-places of Fitzgeralds, Malloys, O'Malleys, and Durnions.

The priest threads the narrow, well-worn dirt path hugging the church to the rectory. Mrs. Dudley has left the light on over the door for him.

He fishes the heavy ring of keys from his trouser pocket, fingers the door key and shakes it free of the others with a bright jingling. He inserts the key and rams the door with his shoulder, but it holds fast.

"Damned humidity," he mutters.

He again twists the key and the handle and rams harder. The door pops open, nearly throwing him into the entry hall. He extracts the key, lets the ring of keys slide back into his left trouser pocket, and is about to slip into the house when he stops and mutters again. "Damn! Mrs. Johnson's gerbil!"

With a sigh, he closes the door behind him and crosses the blank asphalt to the school. The school door opens easily, and the priest disappears inside to feed the pet.

A short, slight man steps out from behind one of the pine trees lining the far end of the parking lot. He stands motionless until a light flashes on behind one of the class-room windows. He begins walking steadily and without hurry across the parking lot. The bell in the church tower begins tolling the hour, and he counts the chimes in his head.

He reaches the door of the school and grasps the handle with his right hand. His left hand grips the hilt of a long knife, the kind a hunter might use to gut a deer.

The schoolhouse door closes silently behind him as the tower bell proclaiming the twelfth hour echoes in the still night air and is gone.

Doug had the coffee perking and the *New York Times* propped up at her place at the table when Mo shuffled into the kitchen on a warm October morning.

One of the advantages of being married to a morning person.

She poured herself a mug of coffee, brought it with her to the table, and settled in with the front section. Reaching out, she picked up the portable radio aligned between the salt and pepper shakers, snapped it on, and set it next to her coffee mug.

"...supposed to be out of bed ten minutes ago, you slug!" an irritating voice told her. "Get up! Time's a–wastin'! This is the old Boomer, Stan the Man, bringing you the local haps, traffic and weather in the a.m. before we get back to your calls."

Frowning, she snapped the radio off, switched it from AM to FM, and tuned it to her public radio station before clicking it on again. The considerably more mellow tones of Steve Inskeep told her it was twenty-one minutes before the hour.

The screen door on the back porch squawked open and slapped shut. Doug stomped the dirt off his sneakers before pushing his way through the back door into the kitchen.

"The world's record for the 10K is safe for another day," he announced, bending to kiss the top of her head.

He toweled off his face and neck with the square of terrycloth he kept on the porch. He picked up the radio and resettled it between the salt and pepper shakers. He walked to the counter and swiped up a spill Mo had made when she poured her coffee.

"Saw two deer up on Presque Isle Road," he said.

He took his water bottle from the refrigerator and straddled the chair across the table from his wife. He took a long swig and let out a satisfied "Aaaah," fanned open his *Wall Street Journal*, and scanned the headlines.

"How was your run?" When he didn't respond, she looked up to find him grinning at her. "What?"

"Nothing. Just basking in my wife's beauty."

"Oh, right. No makeup and pillow hair. What was that you had on the radio?"

"I didn't have the radio on. I never turn it on until you come down."

"Stan the Man?"

He frowned, then nodded. "I listen to the business news while I have my bedtime cup of tea. I must have forgotten to change the station back. Sorry."

"That's okay. Just a little jarring first thing in the morning."

Setting aside the *Wall Street Journal*, Doug fished the sports section out of the *Madison Cardinal-Herald* and took another long swig of water. He folded the paper neatly into quarters, plucked a banana from the bowl on the table, peeled it, folded the peel into his napkin, and took it to the trashcan under the sink.

"What's on your agenda today?" he asked. "You going to hit the 6:30?"

"Yeah. If Mass gets done in time, I'll go to the Chamber breakfast meeting. And after that, another meeting of the Highway Expansion Subcommittee. This afternoon, I've got to get some pictures of the football team practice for the homecoming tab."

"Homecoming already? I didn't even know they'd gone anyplace."

She stood and carried her mug to the counter for one last splash of coffee. At the door, she paused and turned back to him. "I'm sorry I've been so busy lately."

"And when does life get unbusy for a community newspaper editor?"

"Maybe Pierpont will pry open his vault and hire me a reporter."

"Maybe the Cubs will win the World Series."

She hurried upstairs to shower and dress. Doug was digesting his online business reports when she stuck her head in at the door of his office on her way out.

"I'll see you this afternoon."

He turned to smile at her. "Don't forget to eat something."

"I won't."

"Something besides a bag of chips and a cola."

"What's wrong with that? Fiber and caffeine, two of the essential food groups."

He laughed. "You were better off when you ate at Charlie's." He caught himself, frowned. "Sorry. Sore subject. I'll be happy to pack you a lunch."

"Tree bark and prunes? No thanks."

"I don't eat tree bark and prunes. Just good healthy fruits, veggies, and grains."

"It's Monday. Vi will bring bagels. They're good for you, aren't they?"

"Better than donuts, anyway."

She smiled, crossed the room and gave him a lingering kiss. "Gotta go," she said.

"Say a prayer for us heathens."

"I always do."

†††

She'd have to hustle now to get to St. Anne's on time. As she reached the highway, she noted that more hand-painted yard signs had sprouted along the roadside, all expressing shrill opposition to the planned expansion of the two-lane county road between Mitchell and Sun Prairie into a four-lane divided thoroughfare. These homemade protests even outnumbered the store-bought "Support Our Troops" signs.

Two blocks from town, she braked sharply and turned in at the church parking lot, slowing for the gully. Four cars clustered near the front steps. The regulars would already be at their places—Hazel Rose Fenske, Helen Funnell, Martha Molldrum, Eleanor Howery, and Joleen Wodka.

Southern Wisconsin was experiencing a late-season spell of hot, muggy weather. Even so, the little church was cool as she walked up the center aisle, her heels clicking on the wooden floor worn smooth by generations of the faithful coming forward to receive the Body and Blood of Christ. The pew creaked under her, and the unforgiving kneeler cracked the quiet when she lowered it.

Joleen had already finished leading the rosary, but the candles on the altar weren't lit, and the lectionary wasn't on the ambo. Even as she wondered if Father had been abandoned by his altar server, Peter Layonovich appeared at the door behind the altar. He took a hesitant step. His legs folded under him, and he sat with a soft plop.

Mo reached him first, with Hazel and Eleanor right behind her.

"Peter?"

Mo sat next to him on the worn carpeting and put her arm around his shoulder. He started sobbing, his head turned away from her.

"What is it, honey? Do you feel sick?"

Peter sagged against her, giving in to wracking sobs.

"Somebody better go find Father," Hazel said.

Neither she nor Eleanor moved.

Mo squeezed Peter's shoulder, then got up. "You wait here a minute," she said. "I'll be right back. Hazel, will you stay with Peter?"

Something made her pause as she reached the doorway to the sacristy. God be with me, she thought.

Father O'Bannon was lying on his back on the floor, his left arm flung out. His unseeing eyes registered no emotion.

His throat had been slit.

The door of the small wooden cabinet where Father kept the key to the saborium hung open. The lectionary lay open on the counter. Hosts littered the counter and floor. Mo turned and fled.

Hazel sat next to Peter on the carpet behind the altar. Eleanor stood gazing up at the statue of the Blessed Virgin holding the infant Jesus. Helen, Martha, and Joleen sat in their places in the pews. A few others had joined them. They eyed Mo, waiting for her to tell them what to do.

"Don't go back there," Mo heard herself say. "There's been an accident. I'm going to call for help. You all need to stay where you are."

"Hail Mary, full of grace, the Lord is with thee," Joleen

began. "Blessed art thou amongst women, and blessed is the fruit of thy womb, Jesus."

"Holy Mary, mother of God," the others responded. "Pray for us sinners now…"

"And at the hour of our death—" Mo murmured, digging her cell phone out of her purse as she headed quickly for the side door.

2

Mo stood at the back of the church, looking up at the painting of St. Michael the Archangel, sword drawn, doing battle with Satan, when she heard the siren approach from the east. Brakes shrieked, and a car bottomed out in the gully and raced into the parking lot. The siren suddenly ceased. The Harlan's basset, Hildy, bayed in her backyard, and several other dogs howled.

Someone brushed against Mo, and she turned to look into Dilly Nurtleman's troubled eyes.

"Why aren't we having church?"

"Father's had an accident. Somebody's coming to help."

"What happened? Is he all right?"

Mo hesitated. "No, Dill. Father is dead."

Horror spread across the young man's face. She put her arm around his shoulder, and he folded into her embrace.

"What happened to him?" he said into her shoulder.

"I don't know yet."

A short, stocky man pushed open one of the large double doors and poked his head in. "I heard on the scanner you folks got a dead person here," he said in a high voice.

He waddled up the center aisle, looking around as if he'd never seen the inside of a church before.

"Roland Kohl, Chief of Police, Prairie Rapids."

"Monona Quinn. I edit the *Mitchell Doings*."

Roland Kohl had a round head topped with a stubble of brown hair. His brown eyes were a touch too close together in his broad, fleshy face. His rumpled khaki uniform had black pocket flaps and black stripes on the shoulders and down the outside of each pant leg. The top button of the shirt was unbuttoned, revealing a white T-shirt. His thick belt held two sets of handcuffs, a billy club, a cell phone and a holster, which Mo assumed held a revolver under its flap.

Roland Kohl glanced from Mo to Dilly and back to Mo. "You the one solved the murder here awhile back?"

"Yeah!" Dilly said. "I helped!"

"Terrible thing." Chief Kohl shook his head. "A murder in a little burg like this. I grew up in this area, lived here all my life, and I don't remember anything like that happening before. Maybe up in Adams-Friendship, but not here."

Hazel approached cautiously and stood behind Dilly. "Officer?" she said. "May we leave now? I'd like to take young Peter home."

"We'd better stay," Mo said. "The sheriff will need to talk to all of us."

"But why...?"

The throaty growl of a big car bore down on the church. The car stopped, and two doors opened and slammed shut simultaneously. A young black woman pushed through the large double doors, followed by Sheriff Roger Repoz in suit and tie, despite the heat the day promised.

Repoz shook his head when he saw Mo. "Trouble," he said, as if it were her name.

"This is Mrs. Monona Quinn," Kohl said.

"We've met," Repoz said.

He was an inch shorter than Mo's 5'5," and lean. He kept his flint-gray hair short and neat, and his reddish-gray mustache looked as if it had just been trimmed with a T-square. He nodded toward the woman standing behind him to his right.

"Detective Lashandra Cooper," he said.

The detective stepped forward to shake Mo's hand. She was several inches taller than the sheriff and solid—not fat, but substantial. She wore a cream blouse and crisp, pressed black slacks, and carried a cream-colored shoulder bag. She wore her hair in cornrows. She had large brown eyes. She wore no makeup and needed none. Her expression indicated that she wished she were someplace else.

"Roland Kohl," the officer said, stepping forward. "Chief of Police, Prairie Rapids."

Repoz gave him a curt nod. "Where is he?" he asked.

"Back here."

Mo turned and almost bumped into Dilly. Hazel stood to the side of the altar. Peter sat on the riser at her feet.

"You stay out here, Dill," she said.

"Should I pray?"

"Yes. Praying would be real good."

Mo bowed her head toward the altar, crossed herself, and led them to the sacristy, where she paused to let Repoz and Cooper enter first. Kohl pushed past her. Repoz squatted down by Father O'Bannon—Mo couldn't yet think of him as 'the body' or 'the victim'—but didn't touch him.

"The altar server discovered the body," Mo said.

"That the slow kid you were talking to?"

"No. That's Dilly."

"Where's the altar server?"

"Waiting with the others."

"You take him." Repoz nodded to Lashandra Cooper.

"Would you introduce me?" she asked Mo.

"Of course."

"What do you want me to do?" Kohl asked.

"Crowd control," Repoz said without smiling.

Peter still sat on the riser, with Hazel hovering over him, making distressed noises.

"Peter?" asked Mo.

The boy looked up. His eyes were dull with shock.

"This is Detective Cooper. She wants to talk with you."

Lashandra Cooper sat on the riser next to him. "I just need to ask you a couple of questions," she said.

Peter's eyes flicked from the detective to Mo, who nodded.

"Maybe you could start by telling me your name."

The detective took a narrow notepad and pencil from her shoulder bag and set the bag beside her on the step.

"Peter Layonovich."

"You'd better spell that for me."

"P-E-T-E-R."

She glanced at him. "The last name," she said.

He spelled it.

"You're in what, eighth grade?"

"Sixth."

"Quinn! I need to talk to you." Without waiting for an answer, Sheriff Repoz turned and disappeared into the sacristy.

"Excuse me, Peter," Mo said. "I'll be right back."

"Throat slit," Repoz told her when she walked in. "Deep cut. No sign of a struggle, except for the wafers on the floor. He'd be getting those for the service, right?""

Mo frowned. "He would have used an unbroken, unconsecrated host for the Mass," she said. "He'd only need these if he ran out of the ones he blessed during the rite."

"It's hardly standing-room-only out there. Is that a typical crowd?"

"For the weekday Mass, yes. Attendance goes up during Lent."

"Just the regulars today? Nobody new?"

"No. Nobody new."

"When did the altar boy discover the body?"

"About 6:40. We were concerned because Father O'Bannon is... was never late for Mass. When I saw Peter come out from the sacristy, he was crying, and I went to find out what was wrong."

"Sacristy?"

"We're standing in it."

"Oh. You see or hear anything unusual before that?"

"No."

"Who else had access to this room?"

"Father didn't have a sacristant—a helper—for the early Mass. He and the server set up. Mrs. Dudley, the house-keeper, has the key. And Bob Burnstien, the maintenance man. I wouldn't think he'd be here this early."

"Was the church locked?"

"They use a private security firm. They would have un-locked the door about five o'clock. But this door should have been locked."

"What's the name of the security firm?"

Mo shook her head. "I could find out."

"That's okay. When did you last see Father O'Bannon?"

"Yesterday morning at Mass."

"Anybody have it in for him?"

"Not that I know of."

"Nobody was mad at him?"

"Just the typical parish battles."

"Like what?"

"A lot of folks don't think the parish can afford to run a school. And some of the CCD parents feel that their kids are treated as second class citizens."

"The what parents?"

"Many of the parents who don't enroll their kids in the Catholic school send them here once a week for religious instruction. CCD. It's like Sunday School, only on Wednesday nights. The schoolteachers say the CCD kids mess up their classrooms. It's an ongoing war in every parish I've ever been in."

Mo heard the staccato clicking of high heels and looked up to see a tall woman with raven hair enter the room. She was slender and stylish, probably early thirties.

"We've got a dead priest here," Repoz told her.

"So I see. Carol Nicks." She offered Mo her hand. "Dane County Coroner. We met a few months ago."

"I remember." Mo accepted the firm handshake.

Carol Nicks bent down next to the body. "He wasn't killed here," she said.

"What makes you say that?" Mo asked.

"Not enough blood," Chief Kohl said.

Sheriff Repoz looked at him as if he'd forgotten Kohl was in the room.

"That's right," Carol Nicks said.

"I'm taking a correspondence course," Kohl said, grinning. "And the deep slash indicates a crime of passion."

"We'd better get to work," Repoz said to Nicks. He turned to Mo. "Tell the others to hang around so we can talk to them."

"Okay."

As Mo stepped back into the church, she noticed Leona Dudley, looking alone and lost. Mo put an arm around the frail woman's shoulders and ushered her away from the sacristy door.

"Where's Father? What's happened?" Mrs. Dudley gripped Mo's arm with both hands.

"There's been an accident, Leona."

The older woman smelled of soap and talc. She wore a clean white apron over a shapeless light blue housedress. Her fuzzy pink slippers were damp from the dew on the grass. Tears trickled down her heavily powdered cheeks.

"Could we go over to the rectory for a few minutes?" Mo asked. "I could use a cup of coffee, if it wouldn't be too much trouble. I can explain everything there."

"Does Father need anything?" She looked toward the sacristy.

"No. He's... No."

Mo piloted Leona Dudley back to the rectory and into the small kitchen, where a pot of coffee gave off its morning aroma and a plate of scrambled eggs, bacon, and English muffins sat getting cold on the counter.

"I always have Father's breakfast ready for him after Mass."

Mo pulled out one of the two chairs at the small Formica-topped table by the window, and Mrs. Dudley slid into it. The cushion gave a soft sigh. She grabbed Mo's hand and pulled her down into the second chair. "Tell me," she said, the tears streaming down her cheeks. "What's happened?"

"Father's had an accident."

Mrs. Dudley dug around in her apron pocket, dragged out an off-white handkerchief, and blew her nose. She began rocking back and forth almost imperceptibly.

Mo took a deep breath, reached out, and took Mrs. Dudley's hands in hers. "Father's dead."

Mrs. Dudley bowed her head, as if absorbing a blow.

"Is there somebody I can call for you?"

Mrs. Dudley shook herself. She turned her ruined face to Mo. "Twenty-seven years," she said. "That's longer than most marriages last, isn't it? Well..." She drew a deep breath and stood, smoothing her apron and dabbing at her eyes with the handkerchief. "I'd better start fixing the food."

Mo started to say that she didn't think they'd need any food just yet but stopped herself. "May I help?" she asked.

Mo was standing at the kitchen sink, peeling and coring an apple, when Lashandra Cooper tapped on the back door and entered the kitchen. Mrs. Dudley stood to Mo's right, rolling out a piecrust between two sheets of waxed paper on the counter.

"Coffee?" Mo asked.

"I can get it."

The detective fished a mug from the drying rack and filled it from the pot.

Mrs. Dudley took a handful of flour from the bin on the counter, lifted the sheet of waxed paper covering the piecrust, and sprinkled flour on the crust before replacing the waxed paper. She rubbed the rest of the flour on the rolling pin and then scratched at her nose, leaving a streak of white. She rolled out the crust until the sheet of waxed paper curled up on the rolling pin.

Mo put the peeled apple in the colander in the sink with several others, put down the peeler, and took Mrs. Dudley gently by the elbow.

"Let's sit down for a moment," she said, and the older woman did so without resistance. "This is Detective Cooper. She needs to ask you a few questions."

Cooper set her mug on the counter, took her notebook from her bag, flipped it open, and paged through several sheets covered with small, precise script.

"We'll need at least ten pies," Mrs. Dudley said. "Everyone just loved Father."

Mo slid into the other chair and took Mrs. Dudley's hand in both of hers.

"You were Father O'Bannon's housekeeper?" Cooper asked.

"For twenty-seven years."

"What were your duties?"

"Oh..." Her eyes scanned the small room. "I do everything for Father." She drew a deep, shuddering breath. "Cook, clean house, do his laundry. The man would say Mass in his bathrobe if I let him."

She squeezed Mo's hands rhymically, probably unaware she was doing so. Mo watched the detective, who seemed to be just the least bit bored.

"I keep track of everything," Leona Dudley said.

"Do you live here at the rectory?"

"Oh, no. Mr. Dudley and I live over across from Fireman's Park."

"What time did you get here this morning?"

"I get his breakfast ready while he says the early Mass."

"And what time is that?"

"I usually start at six."

"Did you see or hear anything unusual this morning?"

"No." Her brow furrowed in concentration. "I don't think so."

"You didn't hear a siren when the policeman came?"

"Oh, yes. I heard that."

Detective Cooper frowned and made a note, her pen jabbing at the paper. "Did you see Father this morning?"

"No." Mrs. Dudley squeezed Mo's hand with surprising force, and Mo squeezed back.

"When was the last time you saw him?"

The tears started again. "Yesterday afternoon. He was going out to dinner."

"Did he say where he was going or who he was going with?"

"Oh, he didn't need to say. He has dinner with Father Kleinsorge every Sunday night, at Jerry's in Prairie Rapids."

"Did Father O'Bannon have any other appointments yesterday, that you know of?"

Mrs. Dudley shook her head. "If he had, I'd know. I keep all his appointments."

"Father didn't keep a separate calendar or appointment book?"

"No. Not Father O'Bannon."

Mrs. Dudley started to sob. Mo put an arm around her and pulled her close. "Maybe you could finish this later?" she asked Detective Cooper.

The detective flipped her notebook closed. "Sure. I'll need to talk to you, too."

"Okay."

Detective Cooper slipped a business card under her coffee mug on the counter. "If you remember anything else, please call me," she said. "I'll let myself out."

"I don't like her," Mrs. Dudley said as soon as Detective Cooper had left.

"I don't think she especially cares for us, either," Mo said. "Why don't you let me take you home now?"

She eased her arm off Mrs. Dudley's shoulders. The distraught woman looked around the kitchen, as if seeing it again after being gone a long time. "There's so much to do. We need to get the food ready."

"We can take care of that later. Maybe I could call Mr. Dudley for you, and he could come and get you."

"No! No," Mrs. Dudley said. "Don't trouble yourself. I'll call him."

Mo stood by the back door, looking out at the church, to give Leona Dudley some privacy with her phone call. An ambulance was parked in front of the church, the back door open. Two other cars had nosed up beside it. An attendant in a white coat appeared at the church door and rolled out a gurney, with another white-coated attendant handling the back. The black bag strapped to the gurney didn't seem large enough to contain a body. The two young attendants lifted the gurney, carried it down the steps, and slid it roughly into the back of the ambulance. One swung the door shut.

Mo watched until the ambulance had driven out of sight.

Leona Dudley was again sitting at the kitchen table.

"Is he coming?" Mo asked, brushing tears from her eyes.

Mrs. Dudley frowned. "Who?"

"Mr. Dudley. Your husband."

"Coming here?"

"Didn't you just call him?"

"Oh. Yes. He's not home right now."

"I'll drive you home then. Is there someone who can stay with you? A neighbor?"

"Martha," Mrs. Dudley said. "I can call Martha."

Mo helped Mrs. Dudley to the car—the poor woman was really sagging now—and drove her through town and out to her small home across the street from the entrance to Fireman's Park.

The lawn was weedy and overgrown, the bushes untrimmed. The screen door sagged on its hinges.

"Do you want me to walk you to the door?"

"No, no. I'll be fine now. I can call Martha."

"You're sure you'll be alright?"

"Yes. Thank you, dear. You've been very kind." Mrs. Dudley gave Mo's hand a quick squeeze.

Mrs. Dudley made her way slowly up the concrete walk to the front door, fished her key out of her handbag, and fumbled it into the lock. When she was safely inside and the door closed behind her, Mo pulled away. As she drove back to the *Doings* office, she had to fight the urge to turn around, go back, and make sure the poor woman was really okay. Something didn't seem right about that house.

She tried to remember if she had ever met Leona Dudley's husband and couldn't recall having seen him.

She took a deep breath. The impact of what she had witnessed was beginning to settle on her heart. She would have to deal with her feelings later. Right now, she had a lot of work to do.

3

When Mo got to the *Doings*, she snapped on her computer and checked her voice mail. Her hand shook as she noted names and numbers on her pad. By the time she hung up the phone, she was trembling.

Viola stood by the desk, a mug of steaming coffee in her hand. "You look like you need a transfusion."

"Thanks."

Taking the mug, Mo spilled coffee on her skirt.

"Oh, fiddle," Vi said. "Cold water. Before the stain sets."

She bustled into the back room and returned with a wet paper towel, which she used to dab at the spots.

Mo took a deep breath. "Father O'Bannon is dead. It looks like somebody killed him."

"Oh, dear Lord." Vi sank into the chair next to Mo's desk. "I heard a siren."

Mo held her hand out, palm up, and Vi dropped the wad of wet paper into it. Mo leaned over and dropped it into the wastebasket on the other side of the desk. "Peter Layonovich found him in the sacristy. Somebody had slit his throat."

Vi slumped in the chair. "My dear Lord."

"The sheriff asked me if Father O'Bannon had any enemies. I couldn't think of any. Can you?"

In the 43 years Viola Meugard had served as receptionist, secretary, classified ad taker, complaint department, and compiler of the weekly "Looking Back" column for the *Mitchell Doings*, she had seen and heard just about everything. Although Lutheran to her core, Vi knew more about St. Anne's Catholic Church than any member of the parish.

"Nobody who'd kill him!" she said. "Some folks didn't like that radio show, but..."

"Radio show?"

"*The Catholic Church Universal.*"

"I've never heard it."

"You've never heard The Little Hour of Virgin Power?" The door banged shut behind Bruce Randall as he headed for the coffeepot.

"Don't tell me you listen to it." Vi said.

Bruce came over, grinning, and sat on the edge of Mo's desk. His bushy brown beard reinforced his resemblance to a bear.

"It's a heck of a lot better than that Bickens maniac on the Madison station. How did that subject come up?"

"Father O'Bannon's dead," Vi said.

"We found him at St. Anne's this morning." Mo watched Bruce's face as he received the news.

"Good God! Why in hell would anybody do that?" Bruce took a swig of his coffee—Mo had never understood how he could drink it so hot—and shook his head. "I hear he gave boring sermons, but that's hardly a capital offense."

"Arthur Schmeiling," Vi said.

"Who's that?" Mo asked.

"He was pretty mad, wasn't he?" Bruce asked.

"But he wouldn't kill anybody." Vi said.

"Who wouldn't?" Mo asked. "Why was he so mad?"

"He should have known better than to even ask," Bruce said.

"Ask what?" Mo said.

"He and Elaine were married at St. Anne's," Vi said.

Mo looked from Bruce to Vi. "What are you two talking about?"

"Father O'Bannon wouldn't marry the Schmeiling girl at St. Anne's," Bruce said. "She was shacking up with her intended."

"I don't blame him," Vi said.

"They found a priest in Madison to do the job, of course. But Daddy was pretty steamed about it. Said he'd never darken the door of St. Anne's again as long as Father O'Bannon was there."

Mo picked up a reporter's pad from her desk and took the pencil from Bruce's hand. "How do you spell 'Schmeiling'?"

"Playing detective again?" Bruce grinned as he lifted his coffee mug to his lips.

"Playing journalist again. S-C-H...?"

"M-I-E-L-I-N-G," Bruce finished.

"E-I," Vi corrected him.

Bruce shoved to his feet. "I'm going to go put the squeeze on Sy Monroe to run a bigger ad."

"Good luck," Vi said. "He's been running that sixteenth of a page for longer than you've been alive."

"Hope springs eternal."

Mo checked her watch. "The council meeting on highway expansion is supposed to start in ten minutes. I guess I'll have to tell them about Father O'Bannon. I don't imagine they'll have the meeting after that."

†††

Mo drove the two miles out county highway KK to the old Mitchell Town Hall. As she pulled into the gravel parking lot, she took a quick inventory of the cars—Jacob Risley's BMW, Dan Weilman's shiny silver Cadillac, Andy Krueger's Chevy SUV, William Heiss's dusty old Volvo, Frankie French's ancient Volkswagen camper van, Martha and Horace Adamski's vintage '57 T-bird, and Wallace Pierpont's battered Ford pickup.

"Well," Andy said from the front of the hall as she walked in. "I was wondering if the press was going to show up."

"You didn't happen to see the good Father wandering in this direction, did you?" Dan asked as Mo crossed the empty hall to the stage. "I hate to start without him."

The floor was littered with wood fragments, and sawdust covered everything. Exposed two–by–four studs marked where carpenters were apparently attempting to shore up the wall of the crumbling old building.

The five members of the town council plus Risley sat around a small table on the stage. Frankie French, in his fringe jacket and leather headband, slouched in a folding metal chair to stage left, his short legs extended in front of him, feet crossed, the long laces of his hiking boots untied.

She stopped at the foot of the stage. "I'm afraid I have terrible news."

Sunlight filtered through the dirty windows, leaving the stage partially in shadow. The men had covered the table with papers, and Risley had set up an easel behind him.

She waited for Frankie French to look up from his paperback book. "Father O'Bannon has been murdered."

"Jesus, Mary, and Joseph," Andy Krueger said, crossing himself.

Dan Weilman half rose and then slumped back, the chair squeaking under him. William Heiss lowered his head, squeezing his eyes shut as if trying to keep the harsh reality from penetrating. Jacob Risley straightened his papers. Wallace Pierpont folded his hands in front of him on the table and waited, watching her. Frankie French folded the corner of a page down in his book and dropped it to the floor next to his chair.

"We found him at the church this morning. His throat... Someone..."

William filled a paper cup with water from the pitcher in the center of the table, got up, and walked to the steps stage left. He stepped down carefully, as if worried about spilling or losing his footing.

"Here." He offered the water to Mo.

"Thank you."

He seemed not to know what to do next, so she led him back up the steps onto the stage. He returned to his chair, and Mo stood to the side of the table while she quickly told them what she knew.

"Good God almighty," Dan said when she had finished. "Two murders in one summer. We might as well be living in Madison."

"It's ghastly," William said.

Mo took the chair Andy offered her.

"I suppose the Sheriff's already been out," Andy said.

"Big deal," Dan said. "Mo solved his last murder for him."

Many at the table had been involved in the story. Dan had seen diner owner Charlie Connell quarreling with Marcus Trevin, the high school's star wrestler, on the night of the murder. William had revealed through his mural at the Mitchell Historical Society the existence of a second basement under the diner, which had once been the Mitchell Brewery. And Andy, through his interest in purchasing the diner from Charlene Connell, Charlie's mother, had given Mo's husband a chance to investigate the diner's finances. They had all supplied pieces of a puzzle that, when completed, had put an unlikely murderer in jail just two months before.

"Well." Andy put his huge hands flat on the table and took an expansive breath. "I don't know about the rest of you, but I feel like I just got gut-punched. I think we'd better postpone this discussion."

"Yeah," Dan said. "Who in hell wants to talk about the highway now?"

"Risley does," Frankie said.

Jacob Risley started to say something, than apparently thought better of it. He scowled as he gathered up his plans and poster boards.

"When?" It was the first word Wallace Pierpont had spoken since Mo had made her announcement.

Andy consulted his palm pilot. "Wednesday's Rotary. Thursday'll probably be the funeral. How does Friday morning suit you?"

There was a rustling of day planners and thrumming of hand computers.

"No good," Dan said.

"I can't make it, either," William said. "There's a State Historical Society meeting in Madison."

"That go all day?" Martha Adamski asked.

"No. We're done by noon."

"How about Friday afternoon, then? We could start about five o' clock. The workers will be done for the day by then, and I guess Horace can get the fish fry started without me."

The others nodded approval.

"How about you, Mr. Risley? Friday afternoon okay with you?"

"I'll be here any time you say." His voice was anything but genial.

"Why meet at all?"

All eyes turned back to Frankie, who tipped back in his chair. His hand fumbled with the empty knife sheath at his belt.

"The state will do whatever it wants to, whether we like it or not. And brother Risley, here, will have all the roads he needs to bring folks out to his condos and his golf course."

Risley glanced at French and turned to dismantle his easel.

"Five o'clock Friday, then," Martha said, whacking a worn-smooth gavel on the table. "Andy, you stood up first, so I'll put you down as having moved adjournment."

"Friday afternoon okay with you?" Wallace Pierpont nodded toward Mo.

"I'll be here. Just try not to make any news. I wouldn't be able to report it until the following Thursday's paper."

"Fat chance of that," Frankie said, bending to pick up his paperback.

As she drove back to town, Mo wondered if there could be any connection between Father O'Bannon's murder and the planned highway expansion. She didn't see how there could be. Nor did she see any possible connection with Charlie Connell's murder. His murderer was in prison, and his motives had been personal and specific to Charlie.

Mo couldn't imagine anyone from the little town with enough rage to want to kill a priest - any priest -let alone a kind, gentle man like Father O'Bannon.

But then again, Charlie had been a kind, gentle man.

Whatever the reason, someone had murdered Father O'Bannon, and Mo had a strong feeling that she would be involved in finding the killer.

4

Tuesdays were always mind numbing. Mo edited copy and fit stories and photos around the ads Bruce had tucked into the sixteen–page layout, while trying to accommodate the last minute changes and notices people brought in.

So far she had managed to pull the weekly miracle together by late Tuesday each week and get it to the printer in Sun Prairie, so she'd have papers to bundle, label, sort, and get to the post office Wednesday afternoon. But this Tuesday was total insanity.

As soon as Mo finished one call, the chirp of the phone signaled another. Some folks had heard about Father O'Bannon and wanted details or reassurance, or just to talk about it. Others didn't know, and it fell to Mo to tell them.

Vi handled calls on the other line from anyone who didn't insist on talking to Mo.

Taking the calls on her headset, Mo edited stories on her computer screen while she talked, acutely aware that, by trying to do two things at once, she wasn't doing a good job with either.

Sometime in late morning, she slid her chair back from the desk and began rotating her shoulders while letting her head loll in slow circles. Vi came over with a full mug of coffee. Both phones immediately chirped.

"Let Mabel get them," Mo said.

'Mabel' was the name they'd given to the voice on the answering machine.

"How are you holding up?" Vi stood behind Mo and massaged her shoulders.

"Oh, that's good." Mo leaned back and closed her eyes. "I feel like we're Crockett and Bowie at the Alamo."

"You'd think these people would know better than to keep calling."

"They're concerned. And scared. And that's what we're here for—to quell rumors."

"I suppose."

"Bruce should be here soon. He can handle the phone for awhile."

"He'll get 'em off the line in a hurry." Vi kneaded the bunched muscles in Mo's shoulders. "Tactful as a punch in the mush, that one."

"When you get a chance, could you dig up everything we've got on Father O? I've pulled something together for this issue, but I want to run a full profile next week."

Vi was in charge of the *Doings'* ancient filing system— eight cabinets full of manila folders stuffed with clippings. Mo planned to have an intern from the high school put everything on computer some day, but so far, some day hadn't come.

Vi patted her on the shoulder and gave a final squeeze. "Father O has his own file," she said. "I'll check under 'St. Anne's,' too."

Mo watched Vi disappear into the back room. What would I do without you? she thought. Over the months, Mo and Vi had exchanged their stories. Vi had been born and raised on a nearby farm. She put herself through business college in Madison and got the job at the *Doings* when she was barely nineteen. She'd seen a dozen editors come and go and had survived the transition from hot to cold type—the *Doings* was among the last newspapers in the state to stop using a linotype—and from cut–and–paste layout to computer pagination.

She did everything that needed doing around the office, usually before Mo even knew to ask, and her proof-reading had saved Mo much embarrassment. Bruce had dubbed her "the catcher of the awry" for her skill.

The light on the phone blinked accusingly, indicating that Mabel had been taking messages. Mo covered the light with a sheaf of papers, but it didn't help. With a sigh, she picked up the headset the next time the phone rang.

"*Doings.* This is Mo."

"Tracy Peppard. St. Anne's school board."

"Of course, Tracy. How are you?"

"Very well, thank you. I know you must be swamped, so I'll keep this short."

His soft, deep voice calmed her. His was the voice of reason when board meetings became contentious. He had a gift for summarizing arguments, offering compromises, and soothing tempers.

"I'm not sure if you knew this, but along with serving as legal counsel for St. Anne's, I was Father O'Bannon's personal attorney. I'm handling his estate."

"It never occurred to me that he'd have an estate to handle. Don't priests take a vow of poverty?"

"Not in this diocese. Just celibacy and obedience. Actually, his estate is quite substantial. Several million dollars."

Mo couldn't have spoken even if she had had something to say.

"His grandfather founded the O'Bannon Coal and Oil Company, which became O'Bannon Real Estate and Development. They own the Northgate mall, several large condominium complexes, the Lorraine Office Building downtown, Janie's Restaurant, and a few other properties I can't bring to mind at the moment."

"I had no idea."

"Few do. Father thought it might be very hard for some to reconcile the notion of great wealth with a priest, and apparently the family didn't advertise that the eldest son was a clergyman."

Mo took a sip of coffee. It was cold and bitter.

"The reading of the will is Thursday afternoon at four, at my office. We're doing it after the funeral for the convenience of those coming from out of town. You're on the list of those he stipulated should attend."

"I'm… Why? As editor of the *Doings*?"

"I wouldn't think so. He lists you by name."

"Father O'Bannon left me something in his will?"

"Yes."

Mo grabbed a pen and jotted the time and place on a piece of copy paper. She pushed the disconnect button, and the phone chirped. She resisted the urge to slam it down.

"*Doings.* This is Mo."

"Lashandra Cooper."

"Yes. How are you?"

"Up to my backside in barracuda. You?"

"Same."

Vi stood with the files pressed to her chest, looking for a place on Mo's desk to deposit them. With a nod of her head Mo indicated the floor next to her chair and mouthed a thank you.

"The coroner puts the time of death between 10 p.m. and 2 a.m.," Lashandra said.

"So he'd been dead for at least four hours when Peter found him."

"Yeah. He was killed in one of the classrooms. The killer wrapped the body in a blanket and hauled it to the church. Does that mean anything to you?"

"No."

"I need to talk to you. I could be out there in forty-five minutes."

"Sure." Her guts tightened as she said it. An interruption would put the barracuda up way past her backside.

"Meet me at the school. Crime Scene has everything they're going to get."

"Sure. Okay."

"It isn't pretty. That kind of wound produces a real gusher."

Mo took a deep breath. "I can handle it."

"Better give me an hour."

The line went dead. Aye, aye, Captain, Mo thought, and then chided herself for thinking it. The woman had a very high-pressure job. She saw a lot of terrible things. Being brusque—or was it downright rude?—was her way of coping.

Mo pushed disconnect, took another deep breath, shook out her hands, and leaned over to scoop up the files Vi had left for her. The phone chirped. It was one chirp too many.

"I'm switching to Mabel," she called to Vi.

"I gave you the file on road expansion, too," Vi called back. "He's in a lot of the stories."

"Thanks."

Mo leafed through the folder marked 'Father O'Bannon,' typing notes into her computer. The oldest clips were yellow and crumbing. In one, a much younger Father O'Bannon, with a full head of curly hair and the same gap-toothed grin, smiled out at her from the picture that accompanied the story of his appointment to St. Anne's.

She discovered that he was born in Madison, the oldest child of a family that would eventually grow to include seven children. He'd had a younger brother, William, killed in Vietnam in 1967, and a sister, Janie, who died at home in 1970.

He'd entered the junior seminary in 1946. Bishop O'Connor, the first bishop after Madison had been made a diocese, ordained him in June of 1952. He served as an associate at Our Lady Queen of Peace parish in Madison and at St. Albert's in Sun Prairie, had been in charge of the Camp Gray Retreat Center for 18 months, and had for seven years been Catholic chaplain at the university hospital. He'd been assigned to St. Anne's in 1976.

And he'd stayed at St. Anne's for the rest of his life. At 71, he had been four years shy of the mandatory diocesan retirement age of 75.

The story made no mention of O'Bannon Real Estate and Development.

The same mug shot grinned out at her from many of the clips, giving the impression that Father O had been ageless. She scanned the confirmations and first communions, the Christmas and Easter pageants, the appointment of new teachers and principals. There had been a string of associate pastors, ending with the resignation of Father Eagleston, an achingly earnest-looking young man, in 1992. Father O had carried the burden alone since then.

It was unusual for a bishop to leave a pastor at a parish for so many years. Mo wondered at that but didn't pursue the thought. She shifted to the file marked 'St. Anne's' and found many of the same clips, along with stories about the construction of the new school in 1966 and the parish hall and gym two years later. What a building fund drive that must have been, she thought.

She worked on the clips until it was time to get over

to the church to meet Lashandra Cooper. She figured an hour at the school, tops, and then she'd come back and edit the community correspondents' columns. Then she'd finish whatever else needed finishing and get the layouts to Sun Prairie as fast as she could. That would have to be fast enough.

As she trotted across the street to the pharmacy to pick up the Madison and Milwaukee papers, she wondered if she should go back for the jacket she kept in the office. A chill wind gusted from the north.

PRIEST SLAIN IN MITCHELL, the banner headline of the *Madison Cardinal-Herald* screamed.

She recrossed the street and went behind the newspaper building to where she parked her Honda del Sol. Driving the three-quarters of a mile to the church, she dreaded what she was about to see. Two months earlier, dealing with the murder of a friend had shaken her to her core. She dreaded having to face another one.

The detective's white Camaro was the only car in the parking lot, which also served as school playground. Lashandra Cooper was leaning against the car, going over her notes. She wore a dark gray parka with the hood pulled over her head.

"Been waiting long?" Mo asked as she swung in behind the car and hopped out.

"Just got here. Aren't you cold?"

"You ain't seen nothing yet. You're not from around here, huh?"

"Baton Rouge, Louisiana. I've been all over. My father was in the military."

"How'd you wind up in Wisconsin?"

"Don't know as I've wound up yet. Can we get to it?" Lashandra nodded toward the school.

"Yeah."

Mo followed the detective, who took short, rapid steps. "Actually," Mo said when they stopped for Detective Cooper to use a passkey on the school door, "I'm surprised you asked me to come along."

"I figured I'd better not go poking around by myself. I know how you people are."

Mo frowned. "You people?"

"Small town folk." She pushed the door open and entered the building, with Mo close behind.

Nothing could have prepared Mo for what she saw next.

She'd been in Cecelia Johnson's classroom once before, to talk to the sixth graders about the role of the community newspaper. Cecelia was one of the veterans who had helped make the transition to an all-lay teaching staff when the Sisters severed their relationship with the school in the early 1980s. She had covered almost every inch of wall space not taken by chalkboards or windows with colorful construction paper, on which she posted pictures from magazines and newspapers, displays of student work, and a chart listing each student's name and achievements. A crucifix hung over the chalkboard at the front of the room, and a small, white statue of Mary stood vigil on Cecelia Johnson's desk. It was a warm, accepting environment.

But Mo entered a different world now.

Dried, cracking blood had pooled on the floor, splattered on the desks and dotted one wall. Several of the desks had been turned over. Books and notepads were scattered across the floor.

Mo heard a scratching noise and turned. A gerbil peered out at her from its cage. Mo thought she remembered that its name was Edgar. She wondered if anyone had fed it and made a mental note to ask Leona Dudley.

"He was stabbed and no doubt died here," Cooper said.

"Obvious signs of a struggle. Tons of fingerprints all over everything, of course, but the lab hasn't come up with anything useful yet. They're still processing and analyzing."

"What was Father O'Bannon doing here so late at night?"

"I was hoping you'd be able to help me with that."

Mo shook her head.

Cooper flipped a couple of pages in her notepad. "A Father Harvard Kleinsorge says he dropped Father O'Bannon off here around midnight. They apparently had a standing Sunday night dinner date. He seems to be the last person to have seen Father O'Bannon alive. Except the killer, of course. Assuming Kleinsorge isn't the killer."

"You think a priest...?"

"Can't rule anybody out. Let's go sit in another classroom."

"Right."

"Can you think of anybody who might have wanted to harm Father O'Bannon?" the detective asked when they'd settled into the too-small desks in the next classroom.

"No."

"You seem awfully sure. You knew him that well?"

"He was my priest."

"Even priests have secrets. What about that housekeeper? Mrs. Dudley?"

"What about her?'

"Did she and the good Father have anything going on?"

"Heavens no."

"It happens."

"No way."

Cooper consulted her notes. "I understand the priest had a pot of money. Folks have been known to kill for such things."

"I don't think many people knew about that. I didn't."

"Oh, I'm sure folks knew, all right." She flipped her notebook shut and leaned forward. "Look, I can tell you don't like me." Before Mo could protest, she hurried on. "That's okay. I'm used to it. Broad comes in from the big city and starts stirring things up, talking trash about the parish priest. And maybe you got a thing about black folk."

"Now, wait a..."

"Hey. No offense. But honey, you're white, and you were raised in America. If you didn't pick up at least a bit of the old race thing, you'd be the first.

"But that's neither here nor there. The point is, we got us a dead priest here, and it's my job to find out who killed him. Maybe you can help me.

"I don't mean to offend you with my questions. With any murder, sex or money is probably at the core. So, I'll ask you again. Can you think of anybody who would benefit from Father O's death?"

Mo willed herself to calm down before answering. "I got a phone call just before yours," she said. "From Tracy Peppard, the executor of Father O'Bannon's estate. He's going to read the will right after the funeral. He said I should be there."

"Good. You can fill me in. Anybody else have a motive that you can think of?"

"Vi, Viola Meugard, told me about a man who was mad because Father O wouldn't marry his daughter at St. Anne's."

Cooper consulted her notes. "Schmeiling," she read. "He's on my list to talk to."

"She also mentioned a radio show..."

"*The Catholic Church Universal.* A Madison attorney, Francis Kunan, helps Father O'Bannon produce it. It airs on several dozen small radio stations in the Midwest, including the one in town here. Father O'Bannon and this Father Kleinsorge taped the shows. Pretty conservative stuff, apparently."

"You're way ahead of me."

"We work fast. Do you know anything about the Latin Mass?"

"I know they went out with Vatican II."

"Not all the way out. Father O'Bannon had been saying one at the home of a Dr. and Mrs. Ortega every Sunday afternoon for years. He had permission from the bishop."

"You think somebody might have killed him for saying Mass in Latin?"

The detective shrugged. "Solving a crime is usually a process of elimination. You keep eliminating people who didn't do it until you're left with the one who did. So far, I haven't eliminated anybody for any reason."

"Sounds about as efficient as editing a weekly newspaper."

Cooper didn't respond to that. "I understand the diocese just got a new bishop," she said. "I wonder how he feels about Latin Masses."

"I suppose he's on your list to interview, too?"

"Nope. Repoz takes the big fish. So..." Again she leveled Mo with a steady gaze, and Mo fought down feelings of intimidation. "What induced you to give up your nice spot with the *Tribune* to move out here to Mayberry, RFD? You must have gotten culture shock moving here from Chicago, huh?"

"It's another planet."

"Don't you find it confining?"

Mo felt as if the detective were prodding her with a blunt stick. "Not really," she said. "We're close to Madison. And with the Internet, I don't feel cut off."

Detective Cooper nodded. She plunked her elbows

on the desk and leaned forward, cradling her chin in her palm. "Father O'Bannon wasn't involved in any scandals? No allegations of fondling little boys? Nothing like that?"

"No. Nothing."

"Anybody else mad at him that you can think of?"

"Jacob Risley, I suppose. He's trying to sell the town on the idea of the state widening the highway through here. Father was battling him pretty hard on it."

"Risley." Frowning, Cooper consulted her notes. "Tell me about that."

"He represents a consortium of investors who bought land just east of here to build condos and a golf course. The highway expansion would obviously be a good thing for them. For all I know, they may have put pressure on the state to fund the project in the first place. Father O figured the expansion would hurt the town. He was especially concerned that the new highway might tear up part of the church cemetery. And I think he just hated the whole idea on general principles. He showed up for every committee meeting to argue against it."

Cooper took notes as Mo talked. She flipped the notebook shut. "Thanks. That's very helpful. If you think of anything else, give me a call."

"I'll try to help any way I can, detective. I won't get in your way."

"Then we'll get along just fine."

Mo doubted that. She thought about Detective Cooper on the short drive back to the office. She'd felt hostility from the moment they met. What was that woman's problem, anyway? Maybe she thought it beneath her to have to work with folks who have cow manure on their boots. Or maybe it was the race thing. What had she said? If you grew up in America, you were bound to be tainted by racial prejudice.

Mo pushed the subject from her mind. At the office, Vi

and Bruce were taking phone calls. Instead of the jumble of files and clips she'd left on the floor, Mo found the clips she hadn't read in a neat pile to the right of her computer.

Bruce ambled over with a fresh mug of coffee. "What can I do to help?"

"Want to help me edit the correspondents' columns?"

"Vi did 'em. I've got them roughed into the layouts, but you need to go over everything and tighten it up."

"God bless you both."

"I'll drive it over to Sun Prairie when we're done if you'd like."

"Are you sure?"

"No problem."

"You are a sweetheart."

"That's what all the women tell me."

"Shall we send out for pizza?"

"I already did."

"I'm buying."

Mo's fingers were already flying over the keys.

"I'll let you work," Bruce said, and strolled back to his desk.

†††

Mo pulled up next to Doug's SUV in front of their 'little house on the prairie,' as he called it, at a few minutes past eleven o' clock that night. She was surprised to see the light on in his office. He was usually in bed by ten and asleep after the first segment of the local news. He got up at four thirty to jog every day, even on the weekends.

"Did you eat?" she asked as she entered the house, locking the door behind her.

"Leftover beans and rice."

She stood in the doorway of his office. He turned from the computer, rose, walked over, and kissed her.

"You're cold."

"It's chilly tonight. What are you working on?"

"I'm playing, actually. Marty is talking about trading Sweeney and Hudson for Maddux."

"I'd jump on it."

"I will, if he makes an official offer. And speaking of baseball, I got a call from Steve Everson today."

"Do I know Steve Everson?"

"He owns the Madison Mavericks."

"The baseball team?"

"The baseball team. You may just be looking at his new CFO. For the team and Everson's sports bar and clothes store."

"Honey, that's wonderful. Does this mean free passes to the luxury boxes?"

He laughed. "You haven't seen Mansfield Park."

"No luxury boxes, huh?"

"It's strictly bring your own seat cushion. But Everson has big plans." He stepped back, keeping his hands on her shoulders. "You looked whipped. Rough day?"

"I couldn't have gotten through it without Vi and Bruce. Bruce is taking the paper to Sun Prairie for me even as we speak."

"Good man."

"The best."

"You okay? About Father O?"

"I don't know what I am. I'm not letting myself think about it yet. He…"

"What?"

"He apparently left me something in his will. The reading is Thursday, after the funeral. Tracy Peppard called to tell me."

"Really? What do you think you'll get, his mother's Rosary and a bundle of holy cards?"

"Actually, it turns out he had money."

"I didn't think priests could... Wait a minute. Are we talking O'Bannon Real Estate and Development?"

"The same."

He whistled and grinned. "I can buy my own baseball team."

"You shouldn't joke about it."

"You're right. Sorry."

"I am whipped," she said. "I'm going upstairs."

"I'll be up in a minute. I just want to check on that trade."

When he came up to bed 15 minutes later, she was already tucked in and watching Letterman. He took off his slacks and dress shirt, hung up the slacks, and put the shirt in the bag to take to the dry cleaners.

"Please wake me when you get up to run," Mo said. "I've got tons to do."

He crawled under the covers next to her. "I will. And again when I get back. And after I make coffee, and..."

She poked him.

"I worry about you," he said. "This will be another tough story to write."

Mo rolled over to face him. She was surprised to find that she wasn't as tired as she'd thought.

"This time," he said, his fingertip softly tracing her lips, "please just write the news. Don't make it."

"I promise."

They made gentle love, then lay side by side, holding hands. Mo sensed Doug sliding immediately toward sleep, a trait she envied. But he suddenly stirred.

"Hey." he said, squeezing her hand. "I almost forgot."

"What?"

"I made the trade. Sweeney and Hudson for Maddux."

Two minutes later he was snoring. Mo had to wait much longer for sleep to find her.

Doug kissed her lightly on the cheek.

"Time to wake up. I'm going out to run."

"Hmmmph."

"Are you waking up?"

"Hmmmmmph!"

"You sure?"

"Sure."

Sometime later, Jackie launched himself onto the bed, curled up behind her knees, and began to purr. Mo swam up through layers of sleep. She smelled the coffee from downstairs, kicked the cover off—she remembered being cold in the night—struggled into her robe and slippers, and staggered downstairs, the cat twining her ankles.

"Jack Roosevelt Robinson, you be careful." she said. "You'll trip me and kill us both."

Mo got her coffee and took it upstairs, where she spent a few moments looking at her "Chicago clothes" hung neatly in the closet. She wondered when she'd ever wear them again. She got into jeans and a cotton blouse—plenty dressy by Mitchell standards—ran a brush through her short blonde hair, applied minimal makeup, and surveyed the results in the mirror. She looked, she decided, like a small–town newspaper editor who in three years would turn forty.

Mo got into Doug's SUV, which she took on Wednesdays to pick up the papers, and aimed it down the county road toward town. She soon got stuck behind a farmer driving his tractor with a manure spreader trailing behind from the barn to the field. Better keep plenty of distance, she cautioned herself, knowing how Doug hated it when the car got dirty. They'd both detested the traffic in Chicago, but she had to admit Chicago didn't have manure spreaders, plows, tractors, or pickup trucks parked cab to cab in the middle of the road while the drivers exchanged crop reports.

Aren't you in a mood this morning? she chided herself.

She said the Our Father and the Creed and prayed for the soul of Father O'Bannon and for all the Church. She prayed for Doug and his children and–although it still gave her a funny feeling in the pit of her stomach–for his ex-wife, prayed for her parents and her twin sister and her family on the farm outside Summersend, Iowa, and for Doug's mother. Finally, she asked God to lift her out of her selfish funk.

She snapped on Doug's radio, and the strains of a vaguely familiar overture filled the car. She switched to AM, where Ronnie Modrell was finishing up the obituaries on WYUU, which meant Swap Shop was next. She scanned the dial and picked up the Madison talk station, where Stan-the-Man Bickens, "a lawsuit just waiting to happen," was holding forth.

"I'll tell you what we ought to do with faggot anti-war pukes like you," he screamed. "We ought to round you all up and ship you over…"

Mo punched another button, got the oldies station, and let the Beach Boys buoy her spirits.

Tom Fontaine, the day-shift foreman at the print shop, helped her carry the bundles of papers out and load them in the back of the SUV and, when that was full, the back-seats and, finally, the passenger seat.

"Better not get any more subscribers," he said, as he did most every week. "You'll need a trailer."

"I should have such problems."

Mo slid in behind the wheel, and Tom closed the door for her. She rolled down the window.

"You're really getting to be a short timer," she said.

"Two months, three weeks, four days, and..." he made an elaborate show of checking his watch— "one hour and twelve minutes. But who's counting?"

"What are you going to do all day when you retire?"

"Drive Mary nuts."

She smiled over the exchange as she headed back out Highway 19 toward Mitchell. But the good feeling got snagged on the banner headline on the top paper in the stack of *Doings* on the seat next to her:

FATHER MICHAEL O'BANNON
FOUND DEAD IN ST. ANNE'S CHURCH

Mo had written a straightforward account, including a quote from Sheriff Repoz allowing that they "suspected foul play." She'd also run a brief obituary in a black box on the front page. It wasn't enough. She planned a full profile with pictures for next week. That wouldn't be enough either.

She was at her desk, working her way through her weekly post-mortem on the *Doings*, when Dilly blew in.

"Hey, Mokwin. Are the papers ready?"

"As ready as they're going to be."

He frumped down on the floor and waited for her to set the wrapped newspapers in front of him. She had come to rely on him to sort the papers by zip code for the post office, a task he performed with uncanny speed and accuracy, barely glancing at the mailing labels before tossing the papers onto the right piles for bagging.

"Dilly, do you know how to spell dairy?"

He smiled at her. "'D-A-I-R-Y.'" His smile broadened. He was very good at spelling, too, and at remembering peoples' breakfast orders and putting mail in the right boxes for Harriet at the post office. Why he couldn't remember how close to stand or how loud to talk or how to put his underwear on by himself was a mystery.

"Look at this." She folded the paper over for him and pointed. He leaned forward, squinting at the page.

"'D-I-A-R-Y'! That's diary! You made a trypo!"

"I made a trypo. I'm sure Gladys Beeckner will be happy to circle it and any others she catches and send them to us."

"Yeah." Dilly nodded happily. "Mokwin?"

"Dilly."

"Father is still dead, right?"

"Yeah, Dill. Once you're dead, you have to stay dead."

"It still makes me hurt when I think about him."

"Me, too, honey."

"Will it stop hurting soon?"

"It's okay to hurt, Dill. It's a good hurt."

"Why do you have to stay dead?" He took a paper from her and tossed it onto its pile.

"That's just the way God set things up."

That answer seemed to satisfy him, bless him. Mo was about out of answers.

They finished in plenty of time, bagged the papers, and with Bruce Randall's help, lugged them over to the post office. Then Mo bought their celebratory peanut butter chocolate chip cookies at the bakery, and they sat out on the curb, munching together.

"You want to go walk by the river?" Dilly asked when they were finished.

"I'd love to, pal. But I promised Mrs. Manley I'd talk to her journalism class."

"Do you need any help?"

"I think I can handle it. It's just talking."

"Okay. I'll help next day."

"I really don't know how I'd make it without you."

"I'm good at sorting."

"You're the best, pal."

Mo drove the mile or so past Fireman's Park to the consolidated Mitchell-Prairie Rapids High School and pulled into the parking lot just as the passing bell rang. She hustled inside the squat brick building, which looked like a factory. The halls were empty. Mo walked between the rows of lockers, some sporting blue and gold stickers admonishing her to "Maim the Mustangs!"

Esther Manley had her charges seated, hands folded neatly on desks, eyes front when Mo walked into the room. Mo almost expected them to jump up and wish her "Good afternoon, Sister" in unison, as she had been taught to do in grade school. Instead, one of the boys in the back row wolf–whistled—she guessed they still called it that—and was rewarded with nervous laughter from his classmates. Mrs. Manley hurried over and gave Mo a bony handshake.

"Thank you so much for coming. We've been looking forward to your visit." She glanced at the class, as if daring anyone to contradict her. "I appreciate your willingness to tell us what the world of the working journalist is really like."

"It's just like in all the old movies," Mo said, smiling at

the class. "Lots of cussing, a bottle of booze in every desk drawer, reporters screaming 'Stop the presses'."

She drew a few uncertain titters. They had never seen any of those movies.

"I've been having them read the *Doings* every week," Mrs. Manley said.

"I hope that has been edifying," Mo said.

Mrs. Manley smiled. "Class," she said. "Ms. Quinn."

Mrs. Manley took her seat behind her desk. She might have been ordered from central casting, with the silver hair pulled back in a bun, the pinched features, and the half-glasses that perched on the bridge of her nose. But Mo had learned to respect this veteran teacher. Mrs. Manley was intelligent and dedicated—to her students as well as to language and literature. She'd taken on the journalism class ten years before, when the school had cut the position of journalism teacher/newspaper advisor, and gamely learned all she could about a field far removed from Julius Caesar and parsing sentences. If she were fighting a losing battle to try to preserve "whom" and abolish the misuse of "hopefully," she did so with humor and good grace.

Mo looked over her audience—smirks, bored stares and, on a few of the front row faces, expectant smiles. The faces were all white, with the exception of two Asians in the front row and a Native American toward the back.

"I used to work for the *Trib* in Chicago," she began. "What would you think would be the major difference between that and editing the *Doings*?"

"You get paid a whole lot less here?"

"You bet," she said when the laughter died down. "And work a whole lot harder. Any other observations?"

"There aren't as many murders in Chicago?"

Nervous laughter.

"Not what I had in mind. In Chicago, I wrote about

people I met only briefly and never saw again. Here, I write about somebody, and next day, I'm standing in line behind them at the Piggly Wiggly."

"She shops the pig!" a backbencher said.

A blonde in the third row—she had to be a cheerleader, unless central casting had messed up—raised her hand cautiously. Mo nodded at her.

"Does that mean you can't write anything bad about people?"

"No, stupid," a boy in the back said. "You can say anything you want, as long as it's true. Isn't that right?"

"You can," Mo said. "But you'd better be able to prove it—here or in Chicago. And you'd also better be sure it's necessary."

"Class. Why don't we let Ms. Quinn deliver her prepared remarks?" Mrs. Manley said in a tone that made it clear the question was rhetorical.

"They're doing fine," Mo said. "What's your name, young man?"

She had made eye contact with the young man in the back row, a solid-looking citizen with wavy black hair and insolent grin.

"Bradley J. Maeder," he said. "Ma'am!"

"Well, Bradley J. Maeder, is there a question you'd like to ask me?"

"Yeah. Are you going to pin this murder on Mrs. Manley?"

Mo looked over at the teacher, who was shaking her head but seemed undismayed.

"How 'bout it, Mrs. Manley?" Mo said. "Did you do it?"

"I have an alibi." Mrs. Manley allowed herself a small smile of satisfaction.

"There you have it, Mr. Maeder. She says she didn't do it."

"And you believe her? Just like that?"

"There's an old saying in journalism, Mr. Maeder. 'If your mother says she loves you, get a second source.'"

"That means you're going to check out her alibi, right?"

"You bet, Mr. Maeder. Other questions?"

"Yeah."

She directed her gaze to a slightly overweight young lady sitting several rows back by the window.

"Yes? Ms...."

"Daudesdil. I want to know what gives you the right to tell people how to think."

"You don't think a community newspaper should run editorials, Ms. Daudesdil?"

"Isn't it bad to answer a question with a question?"

"Why?"

A few laughed. Ms. Daudesdil was not among them.

"I don't tell people how to think," Mo said. "Couldn't if I wanted to."

"But you tell them what to think about."

"I have the same right to express my opinion as anyone else, Ms. Daudesdil, and sometimes an obligation to do so, as long as I keep that opinion separate from the news. And you have the right to read it or ignore it, accept it or reject it. Other questions?"

"We heard you used to work for *Playboy* magazine," a small young man with dreadful acne said.

More nervous laughter.

"Is there a question in there someplace?"

"Yeah. I mean, did you?"

"Yes. I interned at *Playboy* while I was a senior in college. Learned a lot."

"Did you pose for the centerfold?" Bradley J. Maeder asked.

"Like you wouldn't already know," one of his back-row buddies said.

"I did not, Mr. Maeder. Other questions?"

"Serious questions," Mrs. Manley said.

Several hands sawed the air. Mo pointed to a tall, thin young man in a black T-shirt.

"How'd you figure out who killed that diner guy?"

Mo thought about that. "You ever watch a show called Colombo?" she said. "To answer a question with a question." She glanced at Ms. Daudesdil.

"The detective on cable with the beater car and the trenchcoat."

"That's the one. Your name is…?"

The young man colored from prominent Adam's apple to blond hair. "John Redmond, ma'am. Everybody calls me 'Squeak.'"

"Go, Squeak!" somebody said from the back row.

"Should I call you Squeak?"

"I'd prefer John, ma'am."

"And I'd prefer Mo. Okay, John. How does Colombo solve his cases?"

"He asks a lot of dumb questions."

Most of his classmates laughed, and John Redmond flushed again.

"Exactly," Mo said, smiling. "And that's what a good reporter does. You just keep asking dumb questions until you get the answers."

"And you're a good reporter?" Ms. Daudesdil asked.

"Yeah, I am. I keep asking dumb questions, I listen carefully to what people tell me, and I write it down in plain English."

"And you always get a second source, right?" John added.

"You got it."

The questions became tamer and more predictable. How did you get your first job? (Persistence.) How much do journalists get paid? (Not nearly enough.) Do you use the Internet? (You bet.) When the bell rang ending the period, Mo received applause and whistles.

"Did we ask enough dumb questions?"

"You did, Mr. Maeder. And I look forward to getting your stories for the first *Bulldog Beat* in the *Doings*."

"Those stories are due Friday," Mrs. Manley said over the scraping of chairs and stacking of books. "Will the three students interviewing for the internship please stay seated?"

Mo watched the students pour out of the doors at the front and back of the classroom. Several nodded and smiled at her, and Ms. Daudesdil surprised her by thanking her.

When the others had left, three remained—one of the Asian girls in the front row, the cheerleader, and the Native American. Mo had hoped for Mr. Maeder and Ms. Daudesdil.

"Ms. Ng, Ms. Cheever, and Ms. Thundercloud have applied for the internship," Mrs. Manley said. "They are all well qualified." She turned to them. "I'm going to go to the teachers' lounge while Ms. Quinn conducts her interviews. The selection will be entirely up to her. She has read the writing samples you submitted." She turned to Mo. "They're all yours, Ms. Quinn."

"Thank you."

Mrs. Manley gathered up a neat stack of manilla folders from her desk and left.

Mo smiled at her three candidates.

"Who has to go first?" the cheerleader, Ms. Cheever, asked.

"I'd like to have you all stay."

"You're going to interview us all at once?"

"If that's okay with you."

Ms. Cheever shrugged.

"Why don't you all come sit up front?" Mo turned one of the desks around and sat facing Ms. Ng. She waited while Ms. Cheever and Ms. Thundercloud came forward and turned desks into a rough circle.

"Good." Mo took her pad and pencil from her purse and flipped the pad open. "I need you to spell your full names for me. Ms. Cheever?"

"Suzanne Cheever," she said. "C-H-E-E-V-E-R."

"First name."

She looked blank. "You know, Suzanne?"

"S-U-S...?"

"No."

"That's why I always ask."

They spelled their names for her. Ms. Thundercloud spoke so softly, Mo had to ask her to repeat hers.

"I have no doubt that each of you would make a great intern," Mo said. "Ms. Manley speaks highly of you. I only have one question for you. Why do you want to intern at the *Doings*? Ms. Cheever, why don't you start?"

She drew a deep breath. "I plan on making journalism my career. I think it's one of the highest callings to which a person can aspire. I want to make a contribution to society." Ms. Cheever took another breath. "I feel that an internship at the *Doings* would be an invaluable opportunity to learn new skills."

"Are you considering a career in community journalism?"

Ms. Cheever frowned, and Mo thought she might be deciding whether to tell the truth.

"Not really," she said.

"What, then?"

"I'd like to be a television anchorwoman."

"Who do you like?"

"Excuse me?"

"Which anchors do you think do a good job?"

"I don't know. My folks always have the Today Show on in the morning. Katie's pretty good, I guess."

"Thank you, Ms. Cheever. Ms. Ng? How about you?"

Roberta Ng sat with her hands folded on her desk. "I, too, would like to make journalism my life's work. I think democracy can only work if we have an informed electorate."

"I think so, too," Mo said. "You know what Thomas Jefferson said about newspapers, don't you?"

Ms. Ng shook her head. "I didn't know we were supposed to."

"You weren't. He said if he had to choose between having a government or having newspapers, he'd choose newspapers. Of course, his high opinion of the press changed after he became president."

"I see," Ms. Ng said.

"Ms. Thundercloud. Your turn."

Naomi Thundercloud fixed her gaze on a spot on the floor to Mo's right. "I want to write for *News from Indian Country*," she said so quietly, Mo barely heard her.

"Forgive my ignorance. I don't know that publication."

Ms. Thundercloud picked up her backpack, unzipped it, rummaged around, took out a tabloid newspaper, and handed it to Mo.

"Thank you. May I borrow this to read later?"

Ms. Thundercloud nodded.

"Why don't you tell me a little about it?"

Ms. Thundercloud spoke in a flat monotone. The newspaper was published on the Lac Courtes Oreilles reservation near Hayward in northern Wisconsin, she said; a national newspaper dealing with issues of importance to Indians.

"I heard Paul DeMain, the editor, give a talk once," she said. "At a pow wow. He said Indians need to tell their own stories."

"The term 'Indian' surprises me," Mo said. "I thought 'Native American' was considered more appropriate now."

Ms. Thundercloud shrugged. She kept her gaze on the floor. "It doesn't matter. It's just white peoples' words."

"Thank you," Mo shared her smile with the three. "Thank all of you for your interest. I'll make my decision by Friday."

"That's it?" Ms. Cheever asked.

"Yep. Practically painless, huh?"

Mo found Esther Manley sitting alone at a circular table in the center of the teachers' lounge. She had a cup of coffee and was deep into a stack of student papers. "The bane of the English teacher's existence," she said when she saw Mo. "Have a seat. Want some coffee? It's sludge by now."

"I'll get it, thanks."

Mo filled a styrofoam cup from the pot on the counter, plunking a quarter into the glass jar next to it, as directed by the hand-lettered sign. Behind the counter, a bulletin board held notices of staff meetings, the football schedule, an announcement of tryouts for the student production of *The Music Man*, and a flier urging teachers to support their local union. She took a seat opposite Ms. Manley.

"Any keepers?" the teacher asked.

"They're all bright and articulate. You have to cut through the crapola with Ms. Cheever, Ms. Ng had it on autopilot, and getting Ms. Thundercloud to talk is like pulling impacted wisdom teeth."

"What did you think of their writing samples?"

"Ms. Cheever tends toward the florid. Ms. Ng writes with admirable concision and clarity but little passion. Ms. Thundercloud sometimes stumbles but occasionally soars."

"When do you think you'll make your decision?"

"I've made it. It's Ms. Thundercloud."

Mrs. Manley surprised Mo by breaking into a huge grin.

"You approve?"

"I'm delighted. And surprised."

"Why surprised?"

"Most people overlook her."

"She is very quiet."

"A cultural thing, I'm told. We had an inservice in Madison on cultural diversity."

"Did they tell you to call them Native Americans?"

"Oh, yes, indeed."

"Ms. Thundercloud told me the words don't matter. I think she almost let herself smile when she said it."

"Why did you select her?"

"Gut instinct. Doug, my husband, says I rely too much on it."

"As long as he doesn't call it 'women's intuition'."

"He wouldn't dare." Mo took a last sip of bad coffee and stood.

"May I tell them your decision tomorrow?" Ms. Manley stood with her.

"Absolutely."

Ms. Manley smiled, reaching out to take Mo's hand.

"Thank you so much, Ms. Manley."

"Esther. In the teachers' lounge, it's Esther."

"Thank you, Esther. You're doing a great job with them."

"Thank you."

The veteran teacher gave Mo's hand a final squeeze and released her.

Outside, the sun was already well down in the afternoon sky. The days were getting shorter. Even as she thought it, she heard a sound at once foreign and hauntingly familiar. She looked up, shading her eyes. The sound came again, and Mo spotted a single goose, heading more west than south.

"Way too early," she told it, letting her gaze linger on the pale blue sky.

Still, the plaintive feeling of the coming of fall caused her to shiver. She shrugged it off and set off across the parking lot, her waiting car alone now in the back row.

Father Aloysius O'Connor, Bishop of Madison, presided, with Father James Bakken, the Bishop's "personal hat-carrier," as Doug called him, assisting. Brother priests filled the first five rows of St. Anne's, and the Dane County Executive and the Wisconsin State Attorney General were among the mourners who filled the little church to overflowing.

The Bishop spoke of a life of service to Christ and fellow man, including twenty–seven years at St. Anne's. He had known Father O'Bannon only a short time, he admitted, having come from the Diocese of Helena, Montana, only a few months before, when Bishop Edward Dickinson had finally succumbed to complications of diabetes. But in that time, he assured the faithful, he had come to know the priest as a man of deep faith and unshakable integrity. He referred to Father O'Bannon's passing as a tragic loss for the community and the Church.

He didn't say anything about the way Father O died.

At the end of the solemn high Mass, he announced that Father Bakken would tend the flock at St. Anne's until other arrangements could be made. Standing at the Bishop's left hand, Father Bakken nodded.

"He can't be more than thirteen years old," Doug whispered to Mo, who shushed him.

The pallbearers came forward to escort Father O on the short journey to the cemetery adjacent to the church. Freida Haas scared a massive chord out of the old pipe organ, and the congregation launched into the recessional, "How Firm a Foundation." Father O'Bannon left his beloved church for the last time, his flock following sadly.

Doug headed for the parking lot, along with several others, and Mo and the rest of the remnant followed the coffin to Father O's gravesite under a massive oak tree close to the church. Charlie Connell's grave was just up the hill.

Bishop O'Connor offered the prayers. Solemn-faced Harold Mack and his equally solemn-faced son, Harold Mack, Jr., lowered the coffin into the waiting ground. Women snuffled into their handkerchiefs as they drifted back toward the church, where Mrs. Dudley and the auxiliary would have enough food to feed the multitudes.

"You would have lost him soon anyway."

Mo turned to see Wallace Pierpont a step behind her. For the occasion, he had forsaken his dress white shirt, bolo tie, and khaki work pants for blue pinstripes and wingtips. An impressive sweep of silver hair topped his narrow, weathered face. "The new bishop would have transferred him. From what I've read about his activities in Helena, he likes to rotate the troops. No lifetime appointments for him."

Mo wasn't surprised that her boss, a non-practicing Unitarian, if such a thing were possible, would be up on the inside game of the Catholic Church. Along with running what Mo assumed to be the only amusement park in a town of two thousand in the world, and publishing a string of community newspapers—including the *Doings*—he seemed to be remarkably well–read on everything from foreign affairs to football.

"I rather doubt you'll get a full-time pastor to replace him," Pierpont continued. "You'll have to share a priest."

Mo had to admit he was probably right. The Catholic Church had been suffering from a severe priest shortage even before allegations of sexual abuse made further inroads into the ranks. St. Anne's was vulnerable.

"I think I'll skip the starchfest," Pierpont said, abruptly veering off toward the parking lot. Mo was sorry to see him leave. Trying to keep up with his conversational lunges and parries was exhausting but stimulating, and she was flattered that with her he dropped the role of harmless town eccentric he assumed with most of the others.

The bishop said grace and left for Madison, and folks lined up to be fed. The table sagged under platters of sandwiches—ham and cheese on rolls slathered with butter and mayonnaise—bowls of German style potato salad, gelatin rings, three–bean and seven–layer salad, and plates of homemade apple bars, fudge, several kinds of cookies, and apple and pecan pies, and fruitcake.

Mo put enough Jell-O and bean salad on her plate to look sociable, then succumbed to the temptation to garnish it with two peanut butter chocolate chip cookies, flecks of flour still caught in the crossridges from Julia van Dender's fork. She headed for a table with an empty chair among several of the morning Mass regulars, including Mabel Matusak and Joanne Christensen, who hadn't been in the church when Peter had discovered Father's body.

She spotted Charlene Connell at a table across the hall, surrounded by several ladies of the communal crossword at the diner, Sylvia and Sabra Farnum, and Dilly Nurtleman. Charlene's grief was still fresh from the loss of her son, and here she was, sharing the community's new pain. She had no doubt contributed several of the pies.

One table held most of the members of the common council, a second a large contingent from the VFW, and a third most of the Mitchell-Prairie Rapids School Board.

She greeted the others at her table and took the empty metal chair.

"We're all just in a state of shock," Hazel Rose Fenske said.

"I just can't believe it," Helen Funnell added. "Who would do such a thing?"

"He was such a fine man," Martha Molldrum said.

Mo nodded as Eleanor Howery, Joleen Wodka, and the others added their own tributes. Mabel Matusak was pronouncing Father O'Bannon "a saint and a martyr to the faith" when a metal chair screeched on the tile floor and Mo turned to look up into the round, grinning face of Joey Hasslebaum.

"But even saints have feet of clay," he said as he plopped a dangerously overloaded paper plate on the table. "Mind if I join you?"

Mo moved her chair over, and Joey sagged onto his chair, grabbed his ham and cheese with both hands, and made half of it disappear. He smiled happily at Mo as he chewed.

"Glad to see you folks haven't let all that nonsense about cholesterol scare you," he said when his mouth was not quite empty. "You always find the best spreads in church basements."

He turned to Mabel and asked her about her latest quilting project.

Mo read Joey's "Backroads" column in the *Madison Cardinal-Herald* three times a week and knew he spent a lot of time in small-town diners and at church socials, county fairs, and country auctions. The humor in his stories was gentle and marked by a fundamental respect for the people and their way of life. He was one of them.

"So," Joey said, abruptly turning toward Mo as she attempted to get a spoonful of Jell-O while avoiding the whipped cream. "Is Mitchell trying to replace Adams-Friendship as the murder capital of the Midwest?"

"So it would seem."

Joey shoveled a forkful of apple pie into his mouth, his eyes crinkling at the corners as he chewed. "Any idea who killed the saintly priest?"

Mo shook her head. "I'm surprised they put you on the story."

"They didn't. It's Mayer's beat. I'm just looking for human interest. How the locals are holding up after two murders in three months. That sort of thing."

"How are we holding up?"

"With characteristic Midwestern grit, I'd say. What's your theory on the murder?"

"I don't really have one."

"Maybe somebody had it in for Holy Mother the Church." The remaining pie went into Joey's mouth. "Judging from the artwork."

Mo's expression made him stop chewing. He swallowed hard, choked, and grabbed his water glass. Mo had to stifle the urge to pound him on the back.

"You hadn't heard?" he said when he could talk.

"Heard what?"

Joey looked uncomfortable. "Somebody carved a cross on Father's chest."

Now it was Mo's turn to nearly choke.

"Sorry to be the bearer," he said. "I figured you knew."

"How awful."

"We've got a real sicko on our hands. I'll bet the new

padre sleeps with one eye open, huh? Who is the new guy, by the way?"

"We don't know yet. Father Bakken will say Mass for us on Sunday, but that's temporary."

Joey looked regretfully at his empty plate. "Well." He put his hands on his knees and shoved to his feet with a grunt. "I'd better make tracks. Gotta grind out my seven hundred fifty words. Let me know if anything develops, will you?"

"Sure. You, too."

Mo stayed only a few minutes longer. As she walked out to the parking lot, she was struck by the impulse to turn and walk up the hill to Father's grave instead. As Mo approached the grave, she saw Mrs. Dudley, accompanied by a small man with close-cropped gray hair, wearing a blue suit that still had the wrinkles from the hanger.

"Who's this now?" the man said, scowling.

Leona Dudley turned. Tears streaked her face, and she was holding a handkerchief to her mouth.

"Albert, this is Monona Quinn. She edits the newspaper. Mrs. Quinn, this is my husband, Albert."

Mo stepped forward, hand extended. Albert Dudley looked at it for a moment as if wondering what it was before taking it in his dry, callused hand and giving it a painful squeeze.

"Albert came back especially for the funeral," Mrs. Dudley said.

Funny, Mo thought. Having scanned the crowd in the church with a reporter's eye, she was fairly sure Mr. Dudley hadn't been among the mourners.

"You're the one that blew the whistle on Hopkins," he said.

"Yep. I'm the one."

"Quite the town hero, huh?"

Leona Dudley tried to take her husband's arm, but he shrugged her off.

"Not at all. Wrong place at the right time, that's all."

"I guess I'm in the minority around here, but I figure the old queen had it coming."

"Albert!"

"Hey, I got a question for you," Albert Dudley pressed on, "long as you're here. Something that's been bothering me."

"Albert, maybe now isn't the..."

He glared at his wife, silencing her.

"What's that, Mr. Dudley?" Mo asked.

"Don't get me wrong. I'm no Simon Pure. My wife will tell you that. But I try to follow the rules, okay? And I figure you, somebody who goes to Mass every day and all, you must try to follow the rules, too."

Mo waited for him to continue.

"The thing is, I thought Catholics weren't allowed to marry anybody who'd been divorced. Am I wrong about that?'

Mrs. Dudley appeared to be ready to join Father O'Bannon in the grave. She'd obviously told her husband a lot about Mo.

"It depends on whom you ask," Mo said. "I believe that strict Catholic doctrine still forbids remarriage after divorce, just as it still forbids any practice of birth control other than the rhythm method."

Albert Dudley grinned. "That's a good one. So, you're one of those cafeteria Catholics, huh? Believe what suits you and let the rest go."

Mo chose her next words carefully. "I believe that all Catholics must follow their consciences and try to determine the will of God in their lives."

"You do, huh? Well, good for you, sister. Good for

you." Albert Dudley glanced at his wife. "If anything was to happen to me, you can bet Mrs. Dudley here wouldn't think about marrying nobody else. Ain't that right?"

Mrs. Dudley kept her eyes averted. She looked thoroughly miserable.

"Let's beat it," her husband said.

Mo watched Albert Dudley steer his wife down the hill to the parking lot, then hurried back to the office, where she entered her notes on the service into the computer and then labored over her profile of Father O. She worked until almost four o' clock with few interruptions, while Vi and Bruce handled calls. Then she walked the block and a half to Tracy Peppard's office.

At the four-way stop, she stood across the street from the diner, which still bore the sign "Charlie's Mitchell Café." It was closed for the day and seemed to be waiting.

In the next block, Mo passed Dan Weilman's Starlite Video, Sylvia Farnum's Hair Apparent, Julia van Dender's Sunshine Bakery, and Andy Krueger's Ace Hardware. At the corner, she looked down toward the river, where Madam T had recently converted the old Le Monde Theater into a tea house and art gallery.

Tracy Peppard's office building stood where Mitchell's only gas station had closed a year ago. Gwendolyn Carey had tried to turn it into a boutique but sold the building to Peppard after four months. It was hard, Mo noted, for a former gas station to look like anything but a gas station.

As she walked up the asphalt path, she felt a twinge of curiosity. She certainly didn't want or expect to inherit anything of value, but she wondered what Father O'Bannon might have left her. Beyond the unfailingly cheerful, optimistic, and prosaic priest she had known at Masses, weddings, funerals, and meetings, she really didn't know him at all.

Sandy Towner was at her post at the reception desk when Mo entered. "They're all in the conference room," she said, nodding toward the door behind her.

"Am I the last one here?"

"Yep. People arrive early for this sort of thing. Go right in. They haven't started."

Mo opened the door cautiously.

"Here she is," Tracy Peppard said, smiling at her. "I believe that's everyone now."

"Sorry I'm late."

"You're not." Tracy checked his watch. "Right on the button, in fact."

A large oval table filled most of the room. Seven of the ten chairs were occupied. Mo took the chair next to Tracy, who stood behind his chair, a trim attaché case on the table in front of him.

Mo recognized three of the seven people at the table: Wallace Pierpont, Martha Adamski, and Leona Dudley. Of the others, one looked to be a younger version of Father O— a brother perhaps. He sat across from Mo, next to a fat, florid man in priestly blacks and collar. A man and a woman in business suits, both trim and middle aged, completed the assembly.

Leona Dudley was sniffling and dabbing at her eyes with a wadded-up handkerchief.

"We'll get started, then." Tracy leaned down, snapped the double catches, opened the attaché, and took out a thin sheaf of papers bound in a blue folder. He put on his reading glasses.

"Father O'Bannon's personal share of the family wealth was being held in trust for him. His estate comes to..." He paused to check the document in his hands. "...just over seven million dollars."

Tracy had a deep, resonant voice. He made a $7 million

estate for a small-town parish priest sound like a daily occurrence. Still, the figure stunned Mo.

Father O'Bannon left all of his monetary assets to charity. As Tracy read through the list—Catholic Relief, St. Vincent De Paul, two anti-abortion organizations, a peace activist group in San Francisco, a parish in Colombo, Guatemala, a convent in North Dakota—Mo detected little reaction in the faces of the others at the table.

The final two financial bequests were much closer to home.

"The sum of one million dollars goes to create an endowment fund for St. Anne's Catholic Church," Tracy read, "to maintain and preserve the buildings and grounds and to create a scholarship fund for St. Anne's school. And finally, five hundred thousand dollars to radio station WYUU, to fund the continued production and airing of *The Catholic Church Universal.*"

Mo glanced at Wallace Pierpont, who caught her glance and nodded. The little radio station was a small part of what some of the locals insisted on calling his media empire.

"Now to Father O'Bannon's personal property." Tracy pushed his glasses up on the bridge of his nose and turned the page.

"To Mrs. Leona Dudley..." Her sniffling, which had been constant and muted, now flared into sobs. Martha Adamski leaned over and put her arm over the woman's shoulders. "... my dear companion and friend, who served me and the Church so faithfully throughout my years at St. Anne's, I leave the Rosary blessed by Our Holy Father and my personal Bible, which has been in my family for four generations."

The chalice he had received at his ordination and most of his personal papers went to Father Kleinsorge. His golf clubs went to Francis Kunan, the trim man in the business suit. His cribbage board and a collection of pipes went to his brother Edward, who smiled and nodded. The other woman at the table, Father O'Bannon's sister Bridgette, received a quilt Father O had bought in Ireland and a few personal family items.

"And to Monona Quinn…" Tracy turned toward her, "I leave my books."

Her first thought, she would ruefully admit to herself later, was where will we put them? Her second was curiosity. She had seen the single floor-to-ceiling bookshelf to the left of the fireplace in Father O'Bannon's study but had never had a chance to scan the titles. Then warm gratitude washed over her at having been remembered by this dear, kind man.

Tracy ended with a few procedural details and dismissed the group with his condolences for their loss. Back in the reception area, Mo felt a hand fall lightly on her shoulder and turned to find Edward O'Bannon standing behind her. A long nose divided his lean face and ended in an improbable bulb. He wore gray wool slacks, a tan corduroy coat, and a rumpled white dress shirt, the top button fastened under a prominent Adam's apple. His pale blue eyes resembled his brother's, except that, where the priest's had always sparked with warmth and interest, Edward O'Bannon's eyes seemed cold and appraising.

"Ms. Quinn, is it?"

"Yes. I'm so very sorry about your brother. He was a wonderful priest and a good friend." When Edward O'Bannon didn't say anything, she added, "I guess he was a cribbage player, too."

Edward O'Bannon smiled. "Not much of one. We played sheepshead mostly. Do you play, Ms. Quinn?"

"I must admit I'd never heard of sheepshead until I moved here."

"From...?"

"Chicago."

He again fell silent. Why had the man initiated a conversation, she wondered, if he had nothing to say. "I didn't know Father smoked a pipe," she said.

"Quit long ago. Just collected them. So." Edward O'Bannon gave a slight nod toward the room they had just left. "Not much motive for murder there, eh? Unless maybe you think those nuns in North Dakota did it for the money." His mouth curled in a smile that didn't touch his eyes. "But there'd be no need of that. He'd have given it all to them eventually."

"You didn't approve of your brother's philanthropy?"

The man sniffed, grabbed the end of his nose and gave it a thorough tugging. "Not my place to approve or disapprove. The money was his to do with as he pleased. You much of a reader, Ms. Quinn?"

"I love to read. I don't do as much as I'd like to."

He shrugged his shoulders, adjusting his coat. "What sorts of things? Real or made up?"

"Both. I especially love good fiction."

"Never had much patience for make believe myself. I suspect you'll enjoy Mike's books. A few surprises there. Well, very nice meeting you."

With that, Edward O'Bannon turned and strode to the door and out into the late afternoon sun.

"Monona? May I have a word with you?"

Tracy was standing in the conference room door.

"Of course."

"Let's use my office."

He led her into the next room, a neat, uncluttered little office dominated by the law books that lined the walls.

Tracy held a chair for her, a gesture that made her feel awkward, and settled in behind his desk. He brought a file folder out of a desk drawer, placed it on the desk, folded his hands on top of it, and met her eyes. "There's something about Father O'Bannon's will that I find troubling," he said without preamble. "I thought perhaps you might give me some insight as to how to proceed."

"If I can."

"Would you like coffee? Tea?"

"I'm fine, thanks."

Tracy inhaled through his nose, drawing himself up. "I have to ask that this conversation be strictly off the record."

Mo nodded.

"Thank you. I know that isn't your usual procedure. I appreciate your making an exception in this case.

"Father Mike made an appointment with me to discuss a change he wanted in the will. Specifically, he wanted to enlarge upon the provision regarding his bequest to St. Anne's Church."

He leaned forward. "Ironically, he had a follow–up appointment for today to look over the draft language I had prepared.

"He wanted to set up some sort of legal protection for the St. Anne's grounds and, specifically, the cemetery that abuts the county highway."

"Against any intrusion from an expansion of the highway."

"Exactly."

"Would something like that hold up in court?"

"It might. I certainly tried to craft the language in such a way that it would. There have been precedents. But one never knows how a judge will rule in a case like this. And, of course, the question may be moot, since the codicil was never incorporated into the will."

He drummed his fingertips on the file folder. "I can

attempt to get the codicil included, on the grounds that it was Father Mike's clear intention. I don't know if anyone in the family would object. I can also just forget about it.

"Either way, I think I should bring it to the attention of the highway expansion committee. It might bear on the committee's deliberations. How do you think the committee would receive the information?"

"I don't think it would change anybody's mind. They're all entrenched on one side or the other. Except for one."

"Mr. Pierpont."

"Yes."

"So, you don't think I should bother the committee with it."

"On the contrary. I think you should."

"Because...?"

"I guess I always come down on the side of full disclosure. And besides, then it would be public record, and I could write about it."

Tracy nodded, smiling. "Good. You've confirmed my inclination. I'll call Martha Adamski and ask to be put on the agenda for the next meeting." He stood, moving out from behind the desk. "Thank you so much," he said, ushering her to the door. "If you'd like to take possession of those books now, I'll have Sandy give you a key to the rectory. The books are in three large boxes in the den."

†††

As Mo walked back to the *Doings*, she tried to digest all that she had learned in the last hour. Receiving Father O'Bannon's books stunned and humbled her. And Edward O'Bannon had hinted that she would be even more surprised when she examined the books themselves.

Father O's attempt to preserve the grounds of old St.

Anne's was less of a surprise, but Tracy Peppard asking her for advice was unprecedented.

She wondered if anybody else had known about Father Mike's plans. It occurred to her that the question of whether the codicil would hold up in court was less important than someone's perception that it might.

Then there was the strange and unsettling conversation with Albert, Leona Dudley's husband. Mo had the sense that he was less a strict Catholic than a man who liked to get in peoples' faces for the sport of it.

Back at the office, she returned her calls, then drove to the rectory and let herself in at the kitchen door with the key Sandy Towner had given her. As she walked the hallway to the den, she had the eerie feeling that someone still lived there.

She paused in the doorway to steady herself. She'd been expecting the den to look as it always did. Maybe she'd even expected to see Father O'Bannon leaning back in his recliner, slippered feet up on the rest, listening to a symphony. The recliner was gone. The bookshelf stood empty. Even the fireplace had been cleaned out.

Trying to get her mind around the finality of the priest's death, Mo crossed the room to the three large cardboard cartons, her name printed in heavy black marking pen on each.

She began to cry. She didn't want the books. She wanted Father O'Bannon to be alive. She wanted the evil that had killed him to vanish from the earth.

She snuffled. This will never do, she told herself. She took a deep breath, took up the top carton, carried it to her car, and stowed it in the trunk. She made two more trips. The trunk took two cartons, and she wedged the third onto the passenger seat. She locked the rectory and drove slowly away, not allowing herself to look back at the empty house.

†††

"So, what'd you get?" Doug asked when she got home. "Relics of the saints? The drafts of all his sermons?" His smile dissolved when he saw the look on her face. "Sorry." He crossed the kitchen and hugged her gently. "That was stupid."

She let him hold her for a moment while she became aware of the wonderful cooking aromas that filled the room.

"Books," she said, gently escaping his embrace.

"What kind of books?"

"Don't know. I've got a car full of them."

"I'll get them."

"Let's wait until after dinner."

"Sure."

He served her lamb kabobs out on the porch.

"We won't be eating out here much longer," he said. "Fall's coming."

As they ate, the sun sank to the horizon, wispy clouds turning purple and yellow in its wake. The phone rang as they were finishing their meal.

"Let it go," Doug said.

"No, I'll get it. Just leave the dishes. I'll get them later."

"I'll carry the books in."

"Thanks."

She hurried to snatch up the kitchen phone.

"Mo?"

She recognized Detective Cooper's voice. "Yeah."

"How'd it go?"

"Not much to report. Father left his money to charity."

"Why'd Peppard want you there?"

"Father O'Bannon left me his books."

"What kind of books?"

"I don't know yet. Doug's bringing them in from the car now.

"I've got some news. We found a knife we're pretty sure is the murder weapon. The killer might have tossed it into a field while making his getaway. There was blood on the blade. The lab's got it now. I'm betting the blood is Father O'Bannon's."

"What do you make of the cross?"

"How'd you hear about that?"

"Joey Hasslebaum."

"I wonder how he got it. We're not releasing that detail. I guess it's released now."

"Do you think it's a hate crime?"

"Aren't all murders hate crimes?"

"Good point. There was one other thing."

"What's that?"

"Before he died, Father O'Bannon had asked his lawyer to draw up a codicil trying to make it impossible for anybody to dig into the St. Anne's cemetery. They hadn't had a chance to officially make it a part of the will, but it exists in draft form."

"Aimed at the highway expansion, of course. Sounds about as useful as if I put in my will that I want the death penalty for anybody who dumps their car ashtrays in the parking lot."

"The lawyer says you never know how a judge will rule until you try the case."

"I suppose. Listen. I'm heading out your way tomorrow morning to interview some folks. You want to meet for breakfast?"

The invitation surprised her. "Sure," she said.

"That diner any good?"

"The best. If you like diners."

"Ten o'clock okay?"

"Ten o'clock it is. I'll see you then."

The detective had already broken the connection.

Doug was sitting on the living room floor, a carton open and books stacked neatly on both sides of him. Mo curled cross-legged next to him and picked up a volume, *The Human Comedy*, by William Saroyan.

"I love this book. I read it years ago," she said.

"In mint condition. Look inside."

She turned the pages carefully. A slip of notebook paper fell out and fluttered to the floor. She stuck it back in. "What am I looking for?"

"It's signed. Mo, it's a signed first edition, in perfect condition."

He handed her another book, William Faulkner's *The Sound and the Fury*.

"I read that in college. I had no idea what was going on, but it still moved me."

"It's a signed first edition, too. Agee's *A Death in the Family*. Hemingway's *The Old Man and the Sea*. Harper Lee's *To Kill a Mockingbird*. All first printings of first editions. Most of them signed."

She picked them up one by one: Zora Neale Hurston's *Their Eyes Were Watching God*, Flannery O'Connor's collected letters, Kurt Vonnegut's *Slaughterhouse Five*, John Steinbeck's *Grapes of Wrath*—not only signed, but with a cartoon.

"Here's one I've never even heard of," he said, frowning at the thin volume he held in his hands. "*The Middle of Midnight*. William Gilmore Beymer. Whittlesey House, 1947. It's pretty banged up. Probably not worth much."

Tears welled up again, and she fought them down. "Doug, we can't just stack these in the basement. We have to take good care of them."

"Mo, these are worth a fortune. The Steinbeck alone is worth tens of thousands of dollars."

"For one book?"

"For one book. Look at this one. A signed *Lonesome Dove*. McMurtry doesn't even sign anymore. Oh." Doug held out an envelope. "This was in the carton."

"Monona Quinn" was written in green ink with a fountain pen on the envelope, which wasn't sealed. Mo opened it and took out a single sheet of lined notebook paper covered with graceful script in the same green ink.

"Aren't you going to read it?"

"I'm afraid to."

"Want me to read it for you?"

"No. I'll do it. 'My dear Monona,'" she began, "'When you read this, I hope to be seeing our Lord face to face at last. One does grow weary after all these years of peering through that glass darkly. Our God always keeps his promises, and I rather suspect where I am now is infinitely better than my poor mind could ever invent.

Operating on the principle that you really can't take it with you, I leave you my most prized possessions.I have never been afflicted with the love of money, and most earthly snares have held little appeal for me. I consider this a great blessing. One thing only have I coveted—these books. They have been, one could say, my thorn in my flesh."

May God have mercy on me.

I give them to you for two reasons. First, you love and respect the written word and revere our storytellers. I know you'll give these a good home."

Second, and most important, I believe you will know to rely on our Lord to help you resist over-prizing these books. They are, after all, mere things, as beautiful as they are.

Yours in Christ, Father Michael O'Bannon.'"

Tears streamed down Mo's cheeks. Doug took the letter from her and held her hand. After a few minutes, he got up, helped her to her feet, and walked her up the stairs. The rest of the books could wait until tomorrow.

The mid-morning regulars were at their posts along the counter when Mo entered the diner the next morning. Dilly spotted her and hurried over as she took the unoccupied table near the window. He flipped her coffee cup over and filled it from the pot he was carrying.

"We got strawberry wheat pancakes."

"I'll have a short stack."

"No butter, syrup, or whipped cream, right?"

"You got it."

"And a fruit cup. No pineapple."

"You're the best, Dilly."

"Yeah." A drop of sweat stung his eye, and he mopped his brow with his forearm.

"That detective from Madison will be joining me," Mo said. "She'll want coffee right away."

"Lashandra Cooper, right?"

"Right."

"What kind of name is that?"

"What do you mean?"

"It sounds funny."

"That's just because nobody around here has one like it."

"Where do they have names like that?"

"Louisiana, I guess. It sounds French, doesn't it?"

"Can black people be French?"

Mo laughed. "Alexandre Dumas was black."

"Who's that?"

"A famous French writer."

"Okay. I'm working now. Bye."

Mo cracked open her *New York Times* and scanned the front page, aware of the noise and bustle around her. The only thing missing from Charlie's was Charlie.

A chorus of hoots erupted from the counter as Mel Jenks pushed his way through the door, stomping his boots and huffing as if he'd just come in off the Arctic tundra.

"Get out while you can, boys," he hollered. "Winter's right on my heels."

"You ain't seen nothing yet," Phil Cranley called back from the counter.

Mel shrugged out of his coat and marched over to his stool, mounting it like a cowboy saddling up. That man didn't enter a room, Mo thought; he assaulted it.

Lashandra Cooper had entered in Mel's wake. She spotted Mo and headed over, Dilly right behind her, coffee-pot in hand. Detective Cooper took the chair across from Mo. Dilly poured her coffee.

"Thanks."

"There's the cream and sugar. You gonna try it?"

"Try what?"

"Potato wreckage!" Dilly put the coffeepot on the table so he could count off the ingredients with his fingers. "Onions, peppers, sausage, mushrooms, mangled eggs..."

"Oh, dear God."

"And pepperjack cheese. And yanks!"

"And yanks would be...?"

"Like hash browns," Mo told her, "only chunkier."

"And you've actually eaten this gut bomb?"

"Sure she has!" Dilly said. "Lots of times."

"It really is delicious."

"Pete makes it almost as good as Charlie did, doesn't he, Mokwin?"

"Almost, Dilly."

"He makes mine without mushrooms. I hate mushrooms." Dilly told Detective Cooper.

"Can he make mine without calories?"

Dilly frowned. "He never puts calories in it."

"Well, in that case, bring it on!" she said with a laugh.

"All right! Are you French?"

Mo cringed.

"French? No! Why?"

"Mokwin said you were French, like Alexandre Dumas. He's a famous writer."

"I didn't say that," Mo said. "Not exactly."

"I'm pretty sure I'm not French. But you never know about these things."

"Okay." Dilly snatched up the coffeepot and hurried away.

"I didn't know Dumas was black," Detective Cooper said, allowing herself a smile.

"I guess that's because in France it didn't make any difference."

"Sure seems to around here. Folks stare at me like they've never seen a black person before."

"It's possible that some of them haven't, except maybe on television."

"Come on. You gotta be kidding me." She shook her head, scanning the room. She nodded toward Dilly, taking orders from the Ladies of the Communal Crossword at the big round table in the center of the room. "Doesn't he ever write the orders down?"

"Can't read or write. But he never gets an order wrong."

"Really?"

"Does the math in his head, too. When we get to the register, he'll know exactly what we owe."

Detective Cooper shook a packet of sugar, tore the top off, and dumped the contents into her coffee, then repeated the process with a second. She took a tentative sip. "Decent," she said.

"Pete grinds the beans fresh every morning, just like Charlie did."

The detective took her notepad out of her shoulder bag and flipped it open. "The knife we found was the murder weapon. It belongs to a Frankie French. They brought him in for questioning this morning."

As soon as Mo heard the name, she formed a picture of Frankie at the highway meeting, the sheath empty on his belt.

"He claims he remembers having the knife last Sunday and hasn't seen it since. He says he figured he'd just misplaced it and that it would turn up eventually."

"Do you believe him?"

Cooper shrugged. "Could have happened that way. If he did do the deed, it doesn't make much sense for him to throw the knife away where we could find it. His family will all say he was home that night. How well do you know this guy?"

"Not very. Just at highway expansion committee meetings."

"Does he strike you as being capable of something like this?"

Mo shook her head.

"How come?"

"Gut instinct."

"Gut instinct?"

"I rely on it—too much, according to my husband Doug."

"What's he do?"

"Financial analyst. Does this make Frankie a prime suspect?"

"He and Repoz will be spending some time together."

"Has he been charged with anything?"

"Not as of when I left."

Sabra slid an enormous platter in front of Detective Cooper, her potato wreckage with two puffy biscuits on the side.

"If I eat all that, I'll explode."

"Haven't lost a customer in, oh, three or four days." Sabra set down Mo's pancakes and fruit cup.

"Sabra, this is Detective Lashandra Cooper." Mo nodded at her tablemate. "Detective Cooper, Sabra Farnum, half of the fabulous Farnum twins."

"I'm the pretty one," Sabra said. "Syl runs the clip and dip across the street. Enjoy."

Sabra sashayed back to the counter. Detective Cooper looked up from the steaming platter in front of her. "Was that a cobra I saw snuggling up to our waitress's ear?"

"Yep. Sylvia's got one just like it, only on the other side. One of them used to date a tattoo artist in Madison."

The detective picked up her fork with her left hand and jabbed it into the mound of food. "Kind of bland."

"I guess you're used to Cajun style."

"I'm used to good cooking."

Mo felt her ire rising again and fought it down. This woman was flat-out rude. "I don't hear much Louisiana when you talk."

"We moved when I was seven. I've lived all over."

They attended to their food for a few minutes.

"They got a couple of good prints off the knife," the detective said. "One was Frankie's. They couldn't match the other one. Whoever left it isn't in the system."

"Any other leads?"

"Lots of them. The phone hasn't stopped ringing with folks telling us who did it. Cranks, mostly."

"Anything worth checking out?"

"Probably not, but we have to check them all out anyway." She took a bite of biscuit. "I shouldn't even get started on one of these things. You say the cook's name is Pete?"

Mo told her how Pete the dishwasher, once a suspect in Charlie Connell's murder, had become Pete the chef.

Detective Cooper shook her head. "You folks sure have your ways out here."

"That's twice now!" The angry words were out before Mo could catch them.

"Excuse me?"

"That's the second time you've made a crack about 'you people.' I take that to mean 'small-town hicks.'"

"I didn't mean anything by it."

"You're right. They've got their ways. They're insular, and they don't trust strangers. It's taken me months to cultivate their trust, and I just now feel that I'm starting to be accepted. That means you need me, lady, like it or not, if you expect anybody in this town to open up to you."

Detective Cooper held her hand up. "Whoa. No offense intended."

Mo's heart was pounding. They finished their meal in silence.

"I'm going to go talk to that disgruntled father of the bride," the detective said. "Want to tag along?"

Mo frowned.

"Like you said, I need you. I could use your impressions. And besides, you can tell me how to find the place. I'm meeting him at his home."

"Meeting who?" Sabra stood by the table, coffeepot in hand.

"We need to find the Schmeilings' place," Mo said.

"Head out past the Fun Zone, another mile and a half maybe. When you pass the Hofstedler's place, you're getting close to your turn. It's about one hundred yards past there. Take a left. That's the only way you can turn. That's Deer Run Road, but I think the sign's down. If you get as far as the old motel, you went too far."

"Should I be writing this down?"

"No, no. You're almost there. Go out Deer Run until you cross the river. You'll see a caved-in barn on your right. Pretty soon after that, you'll see the subdivision. The Schmeilings are the third or fourth driveway on the left. There's a Mary in the bathtub as you turn in. Couldn't finish, huh?"

"I could finish. I just wouldn't be able to move."

"I'll get a doggy bag for you. You guys need anything else?"

"We're good, Sabra. Thanks," Mo said.

"Nice meeting you," Lashandra Cooper said.

"You, too. I hope you catch the lowlife who killed the Father. I'm not Catholic, but everybody knows he was good people."

Sabra scooped up the plates and took them back behind the counter. She came back a moment later with a brown bag. "It'll be even better the second day," she said.

Mo slipped two dollar bills on the table and led the way to the counter, where Dilly waited for them at the cash register.

"It's four dollars and thirty-seven cents for you," he told Mo. "And you're three dollars and fifty-three cents," he said to the detective.

"You gotta be kidding. For all that food?"

"I'm buying," Mo said. She turned to the detective. "Your first potato wreckage should be my treat, if that's okay. It's another quaint, small-town custom."

"Seven dollars and ninety cents," Dilly said.

"Thanks," the detective said while Mo fished out the exact change. "I guess I won't pinch you for trying to bribe a cop, just this once."

†††

"I have to warn you, Detective Cooper," Mo said when they had pulled out in the detective's car and were headed east out of town. "Sabra's directions can be a little idiosyncratic, and I've never been out Deer Run Road."

"No problem. That's how we give directions where I come from, too. And can we make it Lashandra? Seeing as how you bought me breakfast and everything."

"Sure."

"How long have you lived here?"

"It'll be a year in November. We moved right after Thanksgiving. Our second night, the temperature dropped belong freezing, and the power went out. I figured they wouldn't find our bodies until spring."

"What happened?"

"I cried myself to sleep, and when I woke up, the power was back on. Doug had a fire going in the fireplace, and it was snowing big, beautiful, fluffy white flakes."

"At least you were used to winter. I'm not sure I'll survive."

"You'll do fine. If we can do it, you can do it. Keep a sleeping bag and a shovel in your car and dress in layers.

Oh, and do not put your tongue on the pump handle, no matter how much the kids dare you."

Lashandra laughed. "Folks have sure got their undies in a bunch about this highway expansion." She nodded toward one of the protest signs at the side of the road.

"Hottest issue in town."

"Does this road go all the way to Milwaukee?"

"Yeah. It used to be the main road before they put in the Interstate."

"When was that?"

"Early 'Sixties."

"Hard to imagine a time before the Interstate, isn't it?"

"Try telling a kid you didn't have a cell phone or a computer when you were growing up. They look at you like you're from another planet."

"Where I came up, you had to wait for your neighbor to get off the line before you could make a call. And then you could be sure they'd still be listening in. Better than TV."

They overshot Deer Run Road, but Mo backtracked and found the Schmeiling home without further trouble. Arthur Schmeiling opened the front door the moment Lashandra knocked. He wore a dark gray business suit, light blue dress shirt, and dark blue tie.

"Come in, Detective. I see you brought the press along with you." Before Mo could respond, he added, "I'm anxious to get this cleared up."

He led them into a large living room with inset bookshelves, an expensive-looking coffee table and end tables, all in pale woods, two large couches that promised little comfort, and an almost total lack of adornment. A large picture window gave out on the front yard, offering a view of a stone-lined pond and several bird feeders near the house.

"Elaine is in Madison for a meeting of the University Women," he said. "I hope that's not a problem."

Mo and Lashandra settled on one of the couches, as unyielding as it looked. He sat on the other couch, facing them. He seemed not to be resting his weight on the seat, so straight was his back, so stiff his arms and legs.

"No problem." Lashandra flipped open her notepad and set it on her knee. "I just need to ask you a couple of questions."

"Do you consider me a suspect?"

Lashandra paged slowly through her notebook, found her place, and looked up, smiling. "Mr. Schmeiling, you find a murderer the same way you diagnose a disease. You eliminate everyone you can until you find the killer."

Arthur Schmeiling nodded. "I see. So you're here to eliminate me."

"In a manner of speaking."

"You're wasting your time. I assure you that an outside criminal element is responsible. Probably some gang-banger from Madison."

Lashandra frowned down at her notes. "It was a local fellow who killed Charlie Connell, though, right?"

He glanced at Mo, then back at the detective. "Can we get on with it? I have a very full day."

"As do I, Mr. Schmeiling. As do I." The detective unclipped a pen from the notebook and began writing. "Let's see. The date today is…"

"October 14."

"Spell your last name for me, please. S-C-H-… ?"

By the time he finished the spelling for her, he was grinding his teeth.

"You have a daughter named Gretchen. Have I got that right?"

"Yes."

"And she recently married a fellow named J.W.... "

"Parker. I know where you're going with this, detective. It's true that Father O'Bannon wouldn't marry my daughter in St. Anne's, because she was cohabitating with this Parker character."

"How did you feel about that?"

"I agreed completely with Father O'Bannon. Nobody disapproved of my daughter's living arrangement more than I did."

"What about Mrs. Schmeiling? Did she disapprove of it, too?"

"Perhaps you think Elaine killed Father O'Bannon?"

"Why should I think a thing like that?"

"You shouldn't. Elaine felt the same way about the situation as I did."

A vein in his temple bulged slightly, and his jaw clenched. When Lashandra remained silent, he added, "She's a wonderful mother, but she's never been able to say no to Gretchen. Not from the day she was born."

"My mama sure didn't have that problem. When was the last time you saw Father O'Bannon?"

"The nine o'clock Mass Sunday morning. She was there." Mr. Schmeiling nodded toward Mo.

"Did you talk with him before or after the Mass?"

"Shook hands with him at the back of the church on the way out."

"Did you say anything?"

"I think I made a comment about the sermon."

"Do you remember what that might have been?"

"Something about how I'd be willing to turn the other cheek if he could convince the terrorists to do the same."

"What did he say to that?"

"He told me to pray for peace."

"That was it?"

"That was it. The business with Gretchen was over and done with, detective. She had a lovely wedding at the campus Catholic center in Madison three months ago."

"You're not upset about it?"

"Look, Father O'Bannon was a man of great faith and high principle, if not the brightest bulb in the marquee. I didn't agree with him on a lot of things, especially the war, but I admired him for having the guts to stick to his guns."

"You and Elaine were married in St. Anne's, weren't you?"

"It will be thirty–five years on February twenty–first. And yes, we would have loved to see Gretchen married in the same church. We also would have loved to see her marry somebody else. I learned long ago that you don't always get what you want."

"Why is that, Mr. Schmeiling? Why would you rather she married someone else?"

He blew air through his nose. "They live in a squalid little room on the east side of Madison, while she puts him through graduate school. He's a fabric artist. He sews buttons on cloth."

Lashandra tucked her pen back into the notepad and flipped it shut. "Thank you so much, Mr. Schmeiling," she said, standing.

"That's it? We're done?"

"For now. I might need to contact you again."

"I'm not going to flee the country, if that's what you mean."

"No, Mr. Schmeiling. That's not what I mean. I want to inconvenience you as little as possible. I know you're a very busy man."

He stood and stepped forward, hand extended. "So, have you eliminated me as a suspect?"

She smiled. "I'm just trying to get as much information as I can, Mr. Schmeiling. You've been very helpful."

†††

"He sells insurance, huh?" Lashandra said when they were back in the car heading down the long driveway.

"Runs his own agency. He's the only game in town, and he works with most of the area farmers, too."

"Is he always that uptight?"

"Whenever I've seen him."

"What does your gut tell you about him?"

"I don't think he did it."

They drove in silence for several minutes.

"Our jobs are a lot alike, don't you think?" Lashandra said. "We both ask people lots of questions and try to figure out what their answers mean. And we both get lied to a lot."

"You more than me, though. I usually put their names in the paper for something good. You put them in jail."

"Not often enough." She negotiated a sharp turn in the road.

"What about you?" Mo asked. "Do you think Arthur was telling the truth?"

"I've learned not to be foolish enough to think I can tell. Some folks are mighty good at lying."

She braked for the stop sign at the highway.

"Frankie French lives not far from here," Mo said. "On up the highway maybe another mile and a half."

"Is that a Sabra mile and a half?"

Mo laughed. "No. That's a Mo mile and a half."

"Do you mind if we swing by, so I can see what the place looks like?"

"Not at all."

Lashandra waited for a car going west to pass by, then

accelerated quickly onto the highway, heading east, away from town.

"Slow down. There. On the left."

Lashandra braked hard. As she swerved onto the shoulder, the car sent up a spray of gravel and shimmied to a stop. Across the road, a narrow dirt driveway snaked into a tangle of pine, maple, and birch trees and a heavy ground cover of vines.

"There's really a house in there?"

"Back up. You can see it from the road."

Glancing in the rear view mirror, Lashandra slammed the car into reverse and floored it. The car shot back and stopped with a lurch.

"That it?"

"Yep."

"I never would have known it was there."

"Frankie likes his privacy."

They were looking at a rustic two-story with a full porch across the front, barely visible through the trees.

"Since he teaches math at the Catholic high school, I assume he's Catholic," Lashandra said.

"It isn't a requirement. He is Catholic, though."

"Married?"

"Very. Eight kids, another on the way."

"Lord today. One of those old-timey Catholics."

"A funny combination of conservative Catholic and aging hippie," Mo said.

Lashandra glanced at the highway and roared off the shoulder, accelerating into a ferocious U-turn.

"And Doug thinks I drive fast."

Lashandra slowed the car slightly as they passed the amusement park and braked sharply as the highway narrowed to become Main Street, downtown Mitchell. "A guy named Pierpont owns that, right?

"Wallace Pierpont. He also owns the *Doings*, the radio station, and a bunch of other toys."

They pulled up in front of the *Doings*.

"Lordy, what a town," Lashandra said. "Two millionaires, one of 'em a priest, in a town of, what, two thousand? And its very own Nancy Drew. Or is it Jessica Fletcher?"

"Neither. Just a hard-working community newspaper editor," Mo said as she got out of the car.

"Keep me posted," the detective said before roaring off.

Mo watched the car speed away. As soon as she reached the town limit, Lashandra floored it, snaking into the first turn and disappearing.

Mo felt bad about blowing up at the diner, but it seemed to have cleared the air between them, so maybe it had been a good thing. At least they were on a first-name basis.

She decided to get a sandwich to eat at her desk while she worked on Father O's profile. As she crossed the road to the diner, something sent a shiver through her—fear, or dread, or both. The last time she'd written about a slain member of the community, her research had led her to the murderer—and almost cost her her own life. Doug wasn't the only one who worried that something like that could happen again.

8

"A little town like Mitchell's got two choices, the way I see it," Andy Krueger said as Mo slipped in through the back door and took a seat in the rear of the dim town hall. "We can grow, or we can die. It's just that simple. You only got to take a look at some of the towns around here to see that's so."

The stage lights were on, but the rest of the auditorium was unlit, with dim sunlight filtering through the dirty windows. Wood scraps littered a floor coated with sawdust. The committee and Jacob Risley sat at the table on the stage, with Frankie French slumped in a chair stage left a few feet away. Mo was surprised to see Frankie.

"Actually, that's not always the case." William Heiss cleared his throat before continuing. "Many small towns maintain a stable population base. Rhinelander comes to mind. It was founded on lumbering and the railroad but survives now with tourism and a few local industries. The population has remained about eight thousand through it all."

"Yeah, and Rhinelander's about eighty miles from

nowhere," Dan Weilman said.. "We gotta try to compete with Madison."

"Rhinelander is forty-five miles from Wausau, actually," William said.

"Like I said, nowhere."

"What's your point, Dan?" Martha Adamski said.

"My point is, we can't count on folks shopping local, when they got Target and Wal-Mart close by."

"And you want to make it easier for them to get there," Frankie said.

"I thought he was supposed to be a silent observer," Andy said.

"You want me to tape his mouth shut?" Martha asked Andy.

"I'd pay money to watch."

Laughter cut the tension.

"We'll certainly allow Mr. Risley to talk," William said.

"Yes, and we used to let Father O'Bannon have his say, too," Wallace Pierpont said.

"I'd think you, of all people, would be foursquare behind the expansion," Dan said. "You stand to gain more than anybody from increased traffic."

"The same road that takes them into Mitchell will take them out," Frankie said. "If I'm still allowed to talk," he added for Andy's benefit. "And which way do you think the young folks are going to want to go?"

"I haven't said I'm against it," Wallace said.

"You haven't said you're for it, either," Dan said. "You've been doing a pretty good balancing act on that fence of yours."

"Which is a good place to be when you're trying to see both sides of an issue," Wallace said.

"That's easy for you to say," Dan said. "You've got more money than the ocean's got salt. But most of us are just trying to squeeze out a living. Us little guys could use some help. Ain't that right, Andy?"

"Gentlemen? Madam chairperson?" They turned toward Jacob Risley, who had gotten up to stand by the easel behind the table. "If I may." He nodded toward Wallace Pierpont. "I think you're quite wise to delay judgment until all the facts are on the table."

He turned to the easel, took down the placard bearing an artist's rendering of the condominiums he proposed to build east of town, and replaced it with a chart covered with numbers. Mo got up and moved to a chair in the first row.

"That's why I keep stressing the numbers," Risley continued. "The numbers do not lie. Construction of the Maunesha River View Condominiums would mean two hundred thirty new jobs for Mitchell and a four-million-dollar infusion into the local economy in the first year alone."

"What jobs?" Frankie perched on the edge of his chair, looking ready to pounce. "The construction jobs will go to some big outfit in Madison. When the thing's built, the locals will get minimum wage jobs flipping burgers."

"A job flipping burgers is better than no job," Andy said. "And jobs'll keep the kids from leaving Mitchell the minute they finish high school."

"Just think for a minute what a highway would do to our town," Frankie said. "The farmland it would tear up. The traffic it would bring through. We'd need a traffic light, maybe two. And more police for the crime that would follow the money. And cheap housing for the folks who'd be cleaning the rich folks' toilets."

"I'm from this town," Risley said. "Most of you know my parents. If I didn't think this development would be good for Mitchell, I wouldn't have anything to do with it."

"Frankie, you talk like these developers are the devil," Dan said.

"First cousins, anyway!" Frankie shouted. "And give the devil his due, Danny boy. We'll get our very own Wal-Mart, and it'll carry a full line of videos and DVDs. They'll sell 'em real cheap, too. And hardware. You think you'll be able to compete with them, Andy? You guys'll be working for them before you know it!"

"Might as well send out for supper, Martha," Andy said in disgust. "Frankie's up on his soapbox, and we'll have to shoot him to get him off it now."

Tracy Peppard slipped into the chair next to Mo. "Did I miss anything?"

"No fistfights. Yet."

Martha Adamski's gavel rapped the table. "Gentlemen, I see that Tracy Peppard has joined us. Why don't you come on up?" she directed at the attorney. "You, too, Mo. Wouldn't want you to miss any of these choice comments."

"Wouldn't matter," Dan muttered. "She just makes the stuff up anyway."

"Your problem isn't that she misquotes you," Andy said. "It's that she prints exactly what you say."

"You requested a place on the agenda today, Tracy," Martha said. "Why don't you have your say right now?"

"Thanks. I'll keep it short."

"That'll be the day," Dan said, "when a lawyer keeps anything short."

Tracy remained standing as Mo slid out a metal folding chair and sat behind and to the side of Martha. Jacob Risley sat down, picked up a pencil and drummed it on the stack of papers in front of him.

Tracy set his attaché case flat on the table. "I don't know if my news will change anyone's mind," he said. "The battle lines seem to be pretty clearly drawn."

"Oh, we're not taking sides," Dan said. "We're all just perched up on the fence with Wally, here."

"Will you quit running your mouth and let the man speak his piece?" Martha said.

"Thank you," Tracy said. "This concerns the provision in Father O'Bannon's will for St. Anne's."

"A sizeable chunk of change, the way I heard it," Dan said.

"One million dollars," Tracy said. "As you know, Father O'Bannon was strongly opposed to any expansion of the highway. His wish was that a portion of his bequest to St. Anne's be used to insure the preservation of the church and grounds, including the cemetery adjacent to the church."

Jacob Risley leaned forward.

"He had planned to strengthen this provision in the will. I had drafted a codicil for him, but he died before he could approve it."

"What does this codicil say?" Dan asked.

"It instructs me as executor of the estate to seek a court injunction against any action that would... let me get the exact language here..." He took a legal-looking document from his case and thumbed to the page he wanted. "... carve so much as a single inch from the existing boundaries of the cemetery."

"He can't do that," Dan said. "Can he?"

"A lawyer can sue anybody for anything anytime," Andy said. "Can and will. The question is, would it hold up in court?"

"How about it, counselor?" Jacob Risley asked. "In your professional opinion, would the court issue such an injunction, and if so, would the injunction hold up on appeal?"

"I quit trying to guess what a judge will do a long time ago," Tracy said. "I believe the matter would go to Chester Bayless's court. Judge Bayless has been quite a strong proponent of property rights."

"Isn't this some kind of church-and-state deal?" Dan pressed.

"The constitution provides for the separation of church and state," Tracy said. "It doesn't take sides on matters of church versus state."

"The state could simply condemn the property and take it," Wallace Pierpont said. "In the public interest."

"That's right!" Frankie said, jumping up. "You're wasting your time even arguing about it."

"Then how come you're pushing us so hard to fight it?" Dan asked.

"Because we shouldn't just lie down and let 'em do it to us!"

"They could seize the property," Tracy said. "I'm sure Mr. Risley here knows of instances in which that has been done."

Jacob Risley nodded once, his face a bland mask.

"But," Wallace Pierpont said, "I'm sure Mr. Risley, and the other business interests involved, would much rather have the community's approval than engender any ill will. Isn't that right, Mr. Risley?"

The developer nodded again. "I would certainly hope, that you, as leaders of the community, would see the wisdom of the proposal I've presented."

"We're the ones has to say if the community's for it or against it," Andy said. "But we don't have any say-so on what the state or a court will do."

"I'm not sure we have any say-so about anything," Martha said.

"That's what I've been trying to tell you!" Frankie hopped up again. "The state's going to do what it wants to. Isn't that right, Risley?"

"The state does exhibit that propensity," Risley said. He turned toward Tracy Peppard. "As I understand it, the discussion is moot anyway. Isn't that so, counselor? You didn't have a chance to incorporate the codicil into the will."

"That's correct," Tracy said. "I think it's quite possible, however, that the judge would accept this document as an expression of Father O'Bannon's wishes. Documents a lot less official than this have held up in court."

Risley's face darkened. Several people started talking at once, and Martha gaveled them down. When she got order restored, the committee tabled the issue and adjourned.

Frankie French fell into step with Mo as they left the building.

"I guess you heard I'm the prime suspect in the murder," he said.

"Detective Cooper told me they'd called you in for questioning."

"It got pretty intense. I mean, they didn't bring out the rubber hoses or anything, but... I can't believe this is happening."

He stopped, and Mo stopped with him. He grabbed the back of his neck and massaged it roughly. "My knife was the murder weapon."

Mo waited for him to say more.

"I explained that I lost the knife, but I'm not sure they bought it. I was home sleeping when the murder happened. That means only my wife and kids can back me up. I can't believe this. I can't believe anybody would think I killed a priest!"

"They have to check out all the angles," Mo said. "They'll get this thing sorted out."

"God, I hope so. I wanted to ask you something."

"Sure."

"You don't know me very well. I mean, we've spoken, what, maybe half a dozen times, if that. All you really know about me is that I'm against the highway expansion, and I'm willing to get in peoples' faces about it."

"I know that you're concerned about the wellbeing of your community and that you're raising a beautiful family. When I see you with your kids in church, you strike me as being a loving and patient father."

"I appreciate that. I really do." His pale green eyes stared at her so intently, she had to fight the urge to look away. "You don't think I could have done this, do you?"

Mo shook her head. "No. No, I don't."

"Thank you. That's… That's all I wanted to ask you."

He turned and walked toward the battered old VW bus he somehow managed to keep running.

Frankie couldn't have done it, knife or not, Mo reflected as she drove back to the *Doings*. He might be a hothead, and out of the mainstream in many ways, but he didn't seem capable of slitting a priest's throat.

Still, Mo had to caution herself. From what she understood, murderers seldom conformed to the stereotypes of pulp fiction. They usually turned out to be plain folks, neighbors, even family members of the victim, the type about whom people say, "I can't believe he'd do a thing like this."

But Frankie didn't have a motive for harming Father O. They had, in fact, been allies fighting the highway expansion. Unless Frankie had some personal, or perhaps church-related, dispute with the priest, he just didn't make a good suspect.

That brought her to Jacob Risley—or someone else with an interest in seeing the highway expansion go through. Father O'Bannon had been the most vocal opponent of the proposal and had even attempted to give legal teeth to his efforts to block it. She supposed she couldn't rule that out as a motive for murder.

Then there was Arthur Schmeiling - or any other disgruntled parishioner who had felt wronged by something Father had done or not done. That seemed like a long shot as a motive for murder. People stopped putting money in the collection plate, went to another parish, even left the Church altogether over such disputes. But murder the priest?

Could the murder somehow be connected with Father O'Bannon's participation in the Latin Mass or the conservative radio program he co-produced? The cross—if indeed that's what it was—the murderer had carved into the victim's chest certainly suggested that sort of motive.

She supposed she had to consider the possibility of some sort of dark secret in Father O's life that had led to his brutal killing. But there had been no hint of scandal in anything she had heard or read about him—no allegations of child abuse, no suggestion of an affair to spawn a scorned woman or a jealous husband.

As she pulled into the parking lot behind the VFW hall on Main Street late that afternoon, she tried to put the matter out of her mind. The moment she walked inside, the smell of fried cod and beer assailed her, and the strains of "The Beer Barrel Polka," as rendered by the Mitchell Soon to be Not Very Famous Non-Marching Band, washed over her. The air was thick with cigarette and cigar smoke—Madison's non-smoking ordinances not having spread to Mitchell.

She spied Leona Dudley dishing up potato salad at the buffet and joined her behind the table. Leona nodded but kept her eyes on her work, and they labored shoulder to shoulder without talking except to greet the folks who came through the line.

"Hey, Sylvia," Mo said. "German or regular?"

"I'm going with the baked beans," she shouted over the

band. "Unless I'm mistaken," she added, nodding toward the door, "that good-looking man who just walked in is more than likely looking for you."

Mo looked up to see Doug standing by the door. "I'll be right back," she told Leona, squeezing her arm.

Relief flooded Doug's face when he saw her approaching.

"I'm so glad you decided to come!" she said. "Let's get you some food."

"Do they have anything baked or broiled?"

"Not a chance. Even the coleslaw's deep fat fried. Come on. You need a little grease in your diet."

She shepherded him to the food table, where a young lady Mo recognized from Mrs. Manley's journalism class had taken over for Leona Dudley. Mo began heaping a plate for him.

"Whoa! Whoa! That's plenty," Doug said.

"It just looks like a lot. It's mostly air."

Mo and Doug found seats at one of the long tables, and Mo introduced him around. Doug poked a fork at a lump of greasy cod and sawed off a small piece.

"So." Mo poured coffee for them from the communal pot. "Your first fish fry."

"Yep."

"Admit it. The fish is good."

"I never said the stuff didn't taste good. I just said it will kill you."

She smiled, shaking her head. "Enjoy it. The latest medical research indicates that admitting you like the food doesn't make it any worse for you."

He smiled back. "By the way, I looked through the last carton of books Father O'Bannon left you." He speared a larger hunk of fish and put it in his mouth. "I hit a whole vein of religious stuff. Merton, Aquinas. C.S. Lewis. The Berigans. Cesar Chavez. Dorothy Day."

"Those last three don't seem like the sort of thing a conservative priest would read."

"Maybe he was just being broad-minded. Oh, and you had a phone call. That priest buddy of O'Bannon's."

"Father Kleinsorge?"

"That's the guy."

"What did he say?"

"Said he was returning your call, and yeah, he'd be glad to meet with you tomorrow morning. You should call before ten tonight if you change your plans. Otherwise, he'll be expecting you."

"Good."

"I'm going in to Madison tomorrow. Why don't we go together? You could meet with Kleinsorge while I talk to Steve Everson."

"Is he going to hire you?"

"I think so."

"It would be a perfect fit for you—finance and baseball."

Doug nodded, smiling. But then his smile turned into a frown. "What do you need to see Kleinhorse about? You're not getting messed up in a murder investigation again, are you?"

"It's Kleinsorge. And no way. I'm just getting background for my profile."

"That's what you said about Charlie."

"Doug, I have no intention…"

"I know. But promise me, if you do dig something up, you'll turn it right over to that detective with the attitude. Okay?"

"Scout's honor. Want more? It's all you can eat."

"I've had all I care to eat."

"But you saved room for pie, right? They've got banana cream. Homemade."

Doug groaned. "I'll have to run twenty miles tomorrow."

"You can run to Madison."

"They really have banana cream?"

Mo laughed. "I'll get you a hunk."

"Make it a small one."

"These ladies don't know how to slice small."

Doug was right, she reflected as she headed for the dessert table. She hadn't intended to get involved the first time. No way would she let it happen again. She'd do just as he suggested. Anything faintly resembling a lead in the investigation would go right to Lashandra Cooper. She'd learned her lesson when Charlie's murderer attacked her. This time, she was determined to stay well out of harm's way.

9

"Do you think there's a connection between Father O'Bannon's murder and this highway expansion business?" Doug asked Mo the next morning as they drove to Madison.

"Detective Cooper keeps saying not to rule anything out."

"She getting any easier to be around?"

Mo considered that. "Yeah. We're even on a first-name basis."

Mo had talked Doug into letting her drive them to Madison in the del Sol. The morning promised a little last-gasp-of-summer warmth, and Mo hoped they might pop the top for the drive home.

"She's not ruling out Frankie French, then?"

"Nope. Apparently, the sheriff grilled him pretty hard and told him to keep himself available."

"How about that developer? Risley."

"I don't buy it. Big-time real estate development is a cutthroat business, but the backstabbing is metaphorical. Besides, he couldn't have seen Father O as a serious threat. He had the counsel vote sewed up, despite Father O's opposition. Aside from that, as Frankie keeps pointing out, they don't really need the counsel's approval to go ahead with the project."

"What about the will?"

"I don't know how much of a threat that really represents. Even Tracy couldn't say if it would hold up in court."

"And now it's time for today's obituaries," Ronnie Modrell told them through increasing static on the radio, "brought to you by the Frachetti Funeral Home."

"You want to listen to that lunatic on that Madison station?" Doug asked.

"Stan-the-Man? Let's pass. My stomach's already a little queasy."

They passed the Schuster's Sweet Swishers barn mural, a local landmark.

"It occurred to me that it doesn't really matter whether the provision would hold up in court or not," Mo said.

"How's that?"

"If Risley—or the people he's fronting—thought it was a threat, that might be a motive, whether the perception was valid or not."

"True. But how would Risley get French's knife?"

"Maybe he didn't lose it at home on Sunday, like he thought. Maybe he lost it at the committee meeting. Maybe somebody found it before it was lost."

They were approaching the outskirts of Sun Prairie. Although Mitchell felt a world away from Madison, it really was just a short drive away.

"So, what do you hope to get from this Kleinhorse character?"

"He and Father O grew up together and went to school together all the way through a Master's in theology."

"Our Father O had a Master's? He always struck me as kind of simple."

"Our Father O taught at the Pontifical University of St. Thomas Aquinas in Rome."

"I have no idea what that is, but I assume it's impressive."

"Very. He was also executive director of the Thomist Association. Not surprisingly, he was a vocal opponent of Vatican II."

"There's more than one Vatican?"

"The Second Vatican Council. I've told you about it."

"Ah, yes. The flaming radicals who said it was okay for the priest to face the congregation and say the Mass in English."

They entered the east side of Madison, approaching Mansfield Park, where Doug was to meet with Steve Everson. She knew Doug was anxious about the meeting, and she prayed it would go well.

"Good luck, sweetie," she said as she dropped him off, leaning over to kiss him before he climbed out of the car.

"Thanks. You, too."

She took her time turning around in the parking lot, watching in the rearview mirror as Doug walked to the trailer that served as the Mavericks' office just outside the ballpark gate. When she saw the door open and Doug disappear inside, she sped off.

She drove into the city past Tenney Park, followed the one-way streets around the Capitol Square, and headed out to the west side. She navigated the last mile by keeping her eye on the spire of the Diocesan Center. The building had until recently served as a high school seminary, but the new bishop closed it, amid great controversy, because of the expense and the lack of production of priests. It had long stood alone in the cornfields, but now condominiums and shopping malls had spread to its eastern border.

Father Kleinsorge met her in the airy foyer fronting

the chapel. He was a large man, shapeless in black pants, coat, and shirt, the tiny strip of white of the priestly collar peeping out from beneath his fleshy chin. He was nearly bald, wisps of unruly gray-brown hair curling around his ears. His eyes were the gray of Lake Michigan on an overcast winter day and peered down at her through wire-rimmed glasses.

"Mrs. Quinn. Good to see you again. You're right on time."

"Thank you so much for meeting with me."

"Not at all. Father Mike was a dear friend. This way, please."

Their footfalls on the smooth tile echoed as he led her down the broad corridor past several closed doors. Only the clicking of her heels and the heavy tread of his shoes broke the silence.

He stopped abruptly, opened a door, and stepped back so she could enter first.

It was an office, she thought, befitting the diocesan canon law expert and top advisor to the bishop—well appointed without being opulent, with floor–to–ceiling bookshelves filled with reference volumes and bound reports. A picture of Pope John Paul II was centered on the wall behind the broad desk, which bore a small lamp, a computer, and a phone/intercom console with touch-tone pad and blinking message light. Tall windows flanked the Pope, with heavy curtains blocking the sunlight.

"Please sit down." Father Kleinsorge indicated an armchair to the left of the desk. "Would you care for coffee or tea?"

"I'd love some coffee."

"Cream and sugar?"

"No, thank you."

He waited for her to be seated before sinking into the

high-backed chair behind the desk. He leaned forward and jabbed at one of the buttons on the phone console.

"Yes?" a woman's voice responded.

"Could you bring coffee for Mrs. Quinn, please? Black."

"Certainly."

A moment later, a thin, middle-aged woman in a tailored gray suit entered through a side door. She carried a cup and saucer with an intricate green, blue and yellow flower pattern. She set them down with a muted clink.

"Thank you," Mo said.

Without glancing at Father Kleinsorge, the woman left through the same door.

"Michael's death was a terrible shock," the priest began without preamble. He seemed to weigh each word before releasing it. "He was a fine man. He had a brilliant mind."

Mo picked the cup up carefully, took a sip, and guided the cup carefully back, even so spilling a bit in the saucer. Father Kleinsorge held out a tissue for her, folded into a square. She lifted the cup and slid the tissue onto the saucer, where it turned dark from the coffee. She took her notebook and pen from her purse, feeling his eyes on her.

"I understand you went to seminary together."

"Junior seminary as well. I actually knew him before that. We went to the same parochial school."

"That was here in Madison?"

"Oh, yes. I'm a native, as was Mike. You no doubt know that his grandfather founded the O'Bannon Coal and Oil Company."

"Yes."

"And you met a brother and sister at the funeral. There was another sister. She died years ago, of ALS. Her death devastated Mike, challenged his faith. They were very close. He was devoted to her throughout her illness."

"I never heard him mention her."

"He seldom talked about her, even with me. He still found it very painful." He waited for her to stop taking notes before resuming. "She was one of the sources, perhaps the prime source, of his passionate defense of Catholic traditionalism. Oh, he was no Hutton Gibson, to be sure, much too rational for that sort of extremism."

"At the risk of sounding completely ignorant, which I am, who is Hutton Gibson?"

"You know the actor, Mel Gibson?"

"Of course."

"Hutton Gibson is his father. A seminary dropout. He's in his 80s now, living in Houston, I believe. Has a new wife perhaps a third his age. He believes that the Second Vatican Council was an anti-Papist Masonic plot, backed by the Jews."

Mo took notes as fast as she could.

"Staunch traditionalists like Hutton Gibson—and I believe his son agrees with him on this—think all the popes going back to John XXIII in the 1950s are not only illegitimate but in fact anti-popes. They base their beliefs and practices on the Council of Trent in the Sixteenth Century and continue to celebrate the Tridentine Mass, the Latin rite. They have several hundred active chapels in America and perhaps one hundred thousand members. Mike was a relatively moderate traditionalist."

"And you?"

"Am I a traditionalist?" Father Kleinsorge leaned back in his chair. "I certainly think Vatican II spawned many excesses. At one point I thought I'd go mad if I had to preside at one more folk guitar Mass. But I don't have a problem with the priest facing the congregation and saying the Mass in their shared language."

He leaned forward and pressed one of the buttons on the phone pad.

"Yes?" the woman's voice said immediately.

"Would you be so good as to bring me my tea now?"

"Of course."

"Thank you so much."

The woman in the tailored suit appeared so quickly, Mo had the sense that she must have been waiting just behind the door, teapot in hand.

"Thank you," Father Kleinsorge said, and the woman again exited without speaking.

Mo waited while the priest poured himself a cup of dark, steaming tea and took a tentative sip. He let out a satisfied sigh, setting the cup in its saucer.

"I'm afraid Mike's doctrinal differences with the new bishop over such matters had already generated some friction between them," he said.

"In what way?"

"The bishop summoned each priest in the diocese for a one-on-one, kind of a get-acquainted chat. Mike was one of the first he called. The bishop informed him that there were to be no more Latin Masses. Mike was thunderstruck."

"The Mass meant that much to him?"

"He certainly believed in it, but I think it was more a matter of how much it meant to the dozen or so who attended regularly. They are a small but extremely devoted group. Mike managed to convince the Bishop to give him a three-month stay of execution, if you will, so folks would have time to get used to the idea."

Father Kleinsorge took another sip of his tea, and Mo drank her coffee, which was velvety smooth. The silent assistant brewed a good cup.

"That must have been hard on him," she said.

Father Kleinsorge nodded. "He didn't complain, but I had the sense that he was caught in the middle of a real crossfire. Some of the faithful apparently felt that he'd buckled under too easily."

"Did you and Father Mike have any disagreements on matters of the faith?"

He arched an eyebrow at the question, and Mo realized that it sounded like something a detective might ask. For a moment, she thought he might decline to answer.

"Father Mike and I were at odds over the Church's doctrine of the just war," he said finally. "Mike was a strict pacifist. He even demonstrated with that lunatic Father Molloy down in Janesville and got himself arrested once or twice."

"I had no idea."

"He didn't believe in mixing his politics with his parish. He thought it important that he be pastor of his whole flock." Father Kleinsorge leaned forward, warming to his subject. "Are you familiar with the doctrine of the seamless garment?"

†††

At that moment, Doug was looking up at what appeared to be the work of a monstrously large spider. Someone had spray painted black sweeps, slashes, and blotches all over the cinderblock walls of the home and visiting team locker rooms in the shadow of the Mansfield Park bleachers.

"The first time, we tried painting over it," Steve Everson told him, "but it showed through. So we sandblasted and repainted. A week later, they hit us again."

The owner of the Madison Mavericks was a short, stocky thirtysomething with a shock of wavy blond hair and a smile that didn't falter even when he was describing the vandalism that had plagued the ballpark for weeks.

"I'm shelling out a lot of money for a security firm,

which the county ought to be paying for in the first place, and they allegedly have somebody here all night, but whoever's doing this is a lot smarter than the pimply-faced kids they hire. I can't believe what they'll strap a gun on and call a security cop these days."

"You've talked to the police, of course."

"Fat lot of good it did me. They told me it was the county's jurisdiction. So I called the Sheriff's Department. They sent out a deputy, who took pictures and asked a lot of questions. He wanted to know if I'd pissed anybody off lately. I told him it would be easier to draw up a list of the people I hadn't pissed off lately."

"Did they turn up anything?"

"If they did, they haven't told me about it."

"What's your theory?"

"Like I say, I've made lots of enemies. I suppose this could have something to do with Sweatshirtgate."

"With...? I'm sorry."

"Don't tell me you haven't heard about that! I caught unholy hell for giving discounts to university athletes on clothes they bought from my store out in Mt. Horeb. Why shouldn't these kids get a break? They bring in huge bucks for the university and get bupkis for it. Everybody cashes in but the guys who actually go out and play the game. Does that seem fair to you?"

"I hadn't given it much thought."

"I don't think the Athletic Department had either, until the NCAA started sniffing around. The university needed a fall guy, and I was it. I caught a raft of shit in the press. There's talk of a full audit."

"That's where I come in."

"That's where you come in. I want you to give the books a good going-over. Talk to anybody you need to talk to. While you're at it, tell me how I can run my operation more efficiently and stop paying so damn much in taxes. Think you can handle that?"

"Absolutely."

"Fantastic." Steve slapped him hard on the back. "Come on. Let's get you a Mavericks team jacket and cap. Unless, of course, you're on an athletic scholarship."

He led the way to the storage room under the grandstand and started rooting through boxes.

"You're going to love these college kids we got playing for us," Steve said. "Most of them know they'll never make it to the major leagues. They just want to play the game for another summer. Baseball the way it was meant to be played! That's our motto."

"How can they play professional ball and still go to college?"

"The players don't get paid in this league. It's all for the love of the game. And to impress the scouts, of course. Here we go."

He stood up, holding a red, white, and blue team jacket. Doug shrugged out of his blue blazer. Steve held the jacket for him, and he slipped it on.

"How does that feel?"

"Fantastic!"

"Looks great on you. Hell, you look like you could still play a little ball yourself. You did play, didn't you?"

"High school and American Legion."

"I'll bet you were a first baseman, tall fellow like you."

"Pitcher, actually."

"This cap should be about right. It's the same kind the players wear. Top of the line."

Doug donned the cap.

"Too snug? That's a seven and an eighth. You might need a seven and a quarter."

"No. This is good. Thanks!"

"Hey, you're a member of the team now, buddy!"

†††

Doug was wearing the jacket and cap, his blue blazer draped over his arm, when Mo pulled up in front of the ballpark gate.

"Look at you." she said as he slipped into the passenger seat. "You made the team!"

He grinned at her. "Do I look too silly?"

"You look wonderful."

"It's going to be great! I can sit up in the press box whenever I want."

Doug talked baseball all the way to Sun Prairie. "But I'm babbling," he said at last. "Tell me about your interview with Father Kleinhorse."

"Kleinsorge. Turns out Father O was an anti-war activist. He subscribed to what Father Kleinsorge calls the doctrine of the seamless garment."

"This has something to do with clothing?"

"It refers to the kind of tunic Jesus wore. They were made out of a single piece of fabric. No seams. That's why the Centurions had to cast lots for it when they crucified Him. They couldn't split it up without destroying it."

"Father O became a pacifist because he didn't want to tear up anybody's tunic?"

"The doctrine of the seamless garment holds that your morality should be consistent—of one piece of cloth, as it were. If you believe that life is sacred from the moment of conception—thus the Church's teaching on abortion—then it's still sacred when it grows up and puts on an army uniform."

"What if it's sitting on death row, waiting to be executed?"

"That, too. Thou shalt not kill applies in all cases."

"I think that's naïve. How about the guy who killed Father O? Do you think he should be allowed to live?"

"I certainly don't believe we have the right to put him to death. Administering the death penalty is cold–blooded, premeditated murder."

Doug was silent for a few minutes. "Okay. How about this? You happen to be there when the guy is about to slit Father O'Bannon's throat. Would you try to stop him?"

"Of course."

"How? By explaining the doctrine of the seamless garment? Suppose you had a gun in your hand, and the only way you could stop him was to shoot him?"

"Come on, Doug. That's ridiculous and you know it."

"It's his life or the Father's. You've got a second to decide. What do you do?"

Anger warmed the back of her neck. "You should have been an attorney."

"Only if I got to be the DA. What's your answer?"

"I don't know! I'm not sure what I'd do. I only know what I think is right."

They drove in silence for awhile. She clicked the radio on. They were close enough to Mitchell to pick up WYUU.

"Nowhere in the Bible," a man said, "does it indicate that you can be saved by faith alone or by simply accepting Jesus Christ as your personal Savior."

Mo gasped. "That's Father O'Bannon!"

Doug reached out to change the station. Mo made a motion to stop him, but stopped halfway.

"I can't listen to this."

Doug turned the dial. Frank Sinatra was singing *Strangers in the Night*. "Reruns," he said, shaking his head. "Life after death." He sang along softly with Sinatra. "I'm sorry," he said. "I didn't mean to press so hard. It's a complicated issue."

"I'm not very rational about it."

"Perfectly understandable."

She eased off the accelerator as they took the long curve past Adamski's Supper Club. Doug was singing along to Dean Martin's *Memories are Made of This*. She wanted to share his good mood, but she couldn't stop thinking about Father O and wondering if he had died for his religious beliefs.

10

It wasn't Pulitzer Prize material, to be sure, but the profile of Father O'Bannon turned out reasonably well, Mo allowed as she performed her weekly autopsy on the *Doings*. She had run a number of pictures of him from his years at St. Anne's and gotten lots of quotes—testimonials, really— from parishioners and other townspeople. The cliché was literally true. She hadn't been able to find anyone with a bad word to say about the man.

She had let Mrs. Dudley have the last word in the article: "Father O'Bannon was as close to a saint as I ever expect to get on this earth."

Poor Mrs. Dudley. When Mo had chatted with her at her home, she seemed to be collapsing into her grief.

Albert Dudley hadn't been home, which Mo figured was just as well, given how unpleasant he had been at their first meeting. He certainly appeared in many of the framed pictures cluttering every horizontal surface and much of the walls of the living room, however. Mo had taken a good look at them when Leona Dudley had gone into the kitchen to answer the phone. In one, he stood next to his wife, his arm around her shoulders in what struck Mo as more a possessive than an affectionate gesture. In others, he posed, grinning, with fellow hunters proudly displaying their deer and other, smaller prey. Mo recognized Frankie French, Horace Adamski, Dan Weilman, and Andy Krueger in the pictures.

She set aside last week's paper and turned to work on the next. Although Father O's memory and influence would endure, in the newspaper business, nothing was as old as last week's story. She had to move on, which in this case included covering the Mitchell-Prairie Rapids homecoming game against Darlington-Pecatonica that night.

†††

Mitchell had blossomed in blue and gold "Maim the Mustangs" placards and banners, and the frightful visage of the Mitchell-Rapids Bulldog glared out from every shop window. At the field, parents and fans filled the home side of the bleachers, and folks backed their pickups along the end zone and sat in the truck beds. The visitors' side bleachers were full of Mustang faithful who had made the trek to cheer on their boys.

The Bulldogs' mighty marching band took the field with a lopsided drum cadence. Ronnie Modrell, doing double duty on the PA and providing the play-by-play on WYUU, asked everyone to stand and observe a moment of silence for Father O'Bannon. Then the band lurched into the National Anthem. The crowd stayed on its feet for the kickoff.

Mo scribbled notes while Doug kept up a running commentary on the game. Despite the exhortations of the crowd, the Mustangs dominated the early going and took a 24-6 lead into halftime.

"You want something from the concession?" Doug asked as they stood to stretch.

"Yes, please. Hot dog. Mustard and onions."

"No ketchup or relish?"

"Perfect. Thank you. And a diet soda."

After Doug left to join the long line, Mo spotted Naomi Thundercloud standing at the low fence at the base of the bleachers. Several clusters of students stood nearby, some leaning over to chat with the cheerleaders, but Naomi stood off by herself.

Mo made her way down the aisle. The two teams were huddling at opposite ends of the field, getting instructions from their coaches. Mo tapped Naomi on the shoulder.

"We still on for tomorrow?"

Naomi nodded, looking past Mo into the stands.

"Have you thought about what topic you want to research?"

Naomi shrugged.

"You'll have more fun if it's a topic you're interested in."

Naomi shrugged again.

"How about high schools with Indian names and logos? That's pretty controversial."

"It's dumb." She was looking at the ground now.

Mo felt the back of her neck getting hot. "You decide, then. I'll pick you up at 8:30. Be sure you're ready. Mr. Hasslebaum is expecting us at 9:30."

†††

But when Mo pulled up in front of the Thunderclouds' small ranch home on the northeastern edge of town the next morning, Naomi wasn't ready. When she finally appeared, clutching her notebook to her chest, her eyes looked everywhere but at the car. Mrs. Thundercloud stood in the doorway, massive in a tent dress, her face an older version of her daughter's passive mask.

"We did a little better in the second half, huh?" Mo said when Naomi was settled in and buckled up.

"They still creamed us."

"True. Did you pick a topic?"

A shrug. It could be a long morning. Mo concentrated on the road as they drove through Mitchell, deserted on a Saturday.

"Would you like to listen to the radio?"

Naomi shrugged again, and Mo admonished herself to stop asking questions that could be shrugged off.

"What would you like to listen to?"

"My father listens to classical music all day."

"Is that what you want to listen to?"

Another shrug. Mo turned the car heater up; there was frost on the pumpkins in McKenzies' field.

"Do you ever listen to that guy in Madison?" Mo ventured. "Bickens?"

"Boomer? All the kids listen to him."

It was by far the most animated response she'd gotten.

"Do you like him?"

"He's okay. He's funny." Naomi watched the farmscape unroll outside her window.

"Have you decided on a topic?"

Shrug.

"Okay. I'll assign one. Find out everything you can about Father O'Bannon." Mo glanced over at Naomi. "Is that okay with you?"

The shrug. Acute shyness? Passive resistance? Disinterest? Maybe all of the above.

Now that she'd assigned a topic, Mo wondered why she'd picked that one. The profile was done. Was she hoping that Naomi would somehow turn up something everyone had missed, some clue that would reveal the killer?

The topic didn't really matter, Mo reminded herself.

The purpose was to let Naomi teach herself how to use the full resources of the Internet for research, with a bit of guidance from Joey Hasslebaum.

They had to wait at the front desk at the *Madison Cardinal-Herald* while the receptionist paged Joey. Behind her, a dozen women sat at their desks. All were talking on telephone headsets while typing. Probably taking ads, Mo figured.

She caught the paunchy security guard looking her over; he turned away under her glare. She walked to the far wall, covered with wooden plaques shaped like the state of Wisconsin. Each represented an award from the Wisconsin Newspaper Association. Joey Hasslebaum had been named "Best Columnist, Class A Circulation Division," in 1991 and again in 1998.

"There you are!" Joey's friendly voice boomed from the stairway. "I'd about given you guys up for dead."

He wore tattered jeans, low under his belly, a soiled white dress shirt, the top two buttons open, and a 1950s-style narrow tie, the knot tugged halfway down his chest.

"Joey," he said, thrusting a hand at Naomi, who seemed to flinch before submitting to a cautious handshake. "I work the dopes, dupes and dolts beat. And you would be…?"

"Naomi."

"Naomi…?"

"Thundercloud."

"All one word? Thundercloud?"

"Uh-huh."

"I think I met your uncle, Joe Rain-in-the-Face."
Nothing.

"You're interning at the *Doings* this semester, right?"
A slight nod.

"Your football team sure stunk it up last night, huh?"
Nothing.

"She'll make a great reporter," Joey said, winking at Mo. "Knows how to keep her mouth shut." Before Mo could answer, he said to Naomi, "I hope you're listening carefully to everything this woman tells you. She's the best."

Mo felt herself blush.

"Get lost, lady," he said to her. "Me and Naomi Speaks Little have work to do."

"Are you sure…?"

"Shoo. Shoo! You'll just contradict everything I tell her. She'd be right, of course," Joey said to Naomi. "But I don't want you to get confused with accurate information while I'm teaching you the Hasslebaum method."

"I'm out of here," Mo said. "Naomi, I'll pick you up at noon, okay? Joey, can you join us for lunch?"

"Love to, but I have to beat it on out to Prairie Rapids to interview a woman who has a collection of political campaign buttons dating back to Rutherford B. Hayes."

††††

Mo drove downtown, actually managing to find a parking space only a few blocks from the Capitol. She walked slowly around the Square, where area farmers and merchants offered late-season produce, baked goods, flowers, honey, and cheeses. There was a definite chill in the air; this would be one of the last Farmers' Markets of the season. She would feel its loss the way Doug felt the end of the baseball season.

Completing her circle of the Capitol Square, Mo crossed the street and entered Shakespeare's Used Bookstore. Usually she headed right for the fiction and mystery sections, but she found herself lingering in front of a locked cabinet of first editions near the counter. Noting the prices, she marveled again at the collection Father O left her. Doug hadn't gotten them appraised, but she knew they were worth a great deal of money.

Would be, that is, if she ever sold them, which she couldn't imagine doing. But if you don't sell them, she asked herself, what exactly will you do with them? Could you actually read a signed first edition?

Possessed by your possessions. That's what Father O'Bannon warned about in his note. He had called the books his "thorn in the flesh."

She paused at the shelf near the door marked "new arrivals" and took down a slim volume titled *The Smoke of Satan,* which turned out to be a discussion of the Conservative Catholic movement in America. Funny how the universe conspired to hand you the very resource you needed, she thought. The price penciled on the first page was little reduced from what the book cost new. Thumbing through, Mo noted that the prose seemed a bit dense. Still, the book might provide some insight into Father O'Bannon's beliefs.

She carried the book to the counter, which was heaped with used books, and handed the book and a twenty-dollar bill to a shaggy man who stood by an ancient cash register. He frowned as he examined both book and currency. His long, gray-brown hair curled in tendrils over his shoulders, and his drooping mustache hid his mouth. Even his eyebrows were overgrown.

He pushed a key on the cash register and fished out her change. He took a small pad and laboriously wrote out a receipt, tearing off the carbon copy for her.

"I figured we'd never sell that one," he said as he dropped coins into her outstretched hand.

"Do you remember who brought it in?"

"The owner does the buying. I just shelve 'em and sell 'em."

†††

The air seemed even colder when Mo stepped back onto the street. She hurried to the YWCA off the Square, arriving just in time for her self-defense class with Suzanne the Warrior Goddess. She got a fairly decent workout, showered and dressed in under an hour. When she walked back through the Square, the crowd had thinned, and snowflakes swirled in a late morning breeze off the lake.

Mo fought the urge to speed as she drove down Park Street to the huge concrete fortress of the *Cardinal-Herald*. Naomi was waiting for her in the lobby, sitting on one of the two plastic chairs, her hands folded over her notebook in her lap. To Mo's shock, she bounced up and almost ran over.

"It was cool! He showed me a web site some Indian kids out in Colorado made. They're selling hats and shirts and stuff for the 'Fighting Whities.' It's, you know, a protest of teams named 'Redskins' and 'Warriors'."

She had words in there all the time, Mo marveled as they got into the car and fastened their seat belts. As she drove them back downtown, Naomi described other sites Joey had showed her and the results they got when they typed Father O'Bannon's name into the newspaper's search engine.

"Where do you want to go to for lunch?" Mo asked when Naomi paused for breath.

"I don't care. McDonald's?"

"I don't do McDonald's. How about a place with food that's really, really good and really, really bad for you?"

Shrug.

Mo found a parking place in a residential area where all the streets were named for presidents, and they walked three blocks to Regent Street, directly across from Camp Randall, the college football stadium.

Mickey's was packed, a crush of people standing just inside the door. When Mo and Naomi finally got a small booth toward the back, a tired-looking waitress confronted them, coffeepot in one hand, the other hand on her hip.

"Chewwan coffee?"

"Yes, please," Mo said.

Naomi nodded, sliding her mug to the edge of the table.

"Cream and sugar's on the table. Chewno whatcha want?"

Mo pointed to the wall above the pass-through to the kitchen, where wooden plaques listed the menu items. Naomi squinted, studying her choices.

"Pancakes," she said.

"One or two?"

"Two."

"They're huge," Mo cautioned.

"Somethun elsta drink?"

"Can I have water?"

"Sure. You?"

"Burger and yanks," Mo said.

"Cheese and onion?"

"Please."

The waitress slid down the line of booths, refilling coffee mugs. Naomi opened and poured two small containers of creamer into her coffee and followed it with three packets of sugar. She stirred vigorously and took a sip, eyes narrowed in concentration.

Their waitress came back with a small glass of water for Naomi.

"Yer food'll be up inna minute."

"So," Mo said when the waitress again left, "Mr. Hasslebaum knows his way around cyberspace, huh?"

"They don't let them smoke in the newsroom." Naomi brought her coffee mug to her mouth with both hands and took another sip. "One guy went outside to smoke lots of times. Cigarettes stink. I'm never going to smoke."

"You're smart."

"You ever smoke?"

"I did. Filthy habit."

"When did you quit?"

"When I got married. My husband's allergic to smoke."

"Was it hard?"

"Awful. I quit cold turkey, no patch, no nothing."

"You ever want to smoke now?"

"Oh, yeah! Sometimes I dream I'm smoking, and when I wake up, I'm not sure I didn't actually do it."

"My parents smoke. It's stupid."

"Here yare."

The waitress slid a platter in front of Naomi. The pancakes looked like a two-layer cake without the frosting. Mo's platter hit the table in front of her—toasted bun, thick, hand-formed beef patty, a pickle spear, and an enormous mound of fried potatoes. A small pitcher of syrup banged the table between them.

"Anything else?"

"I can't imagine what it would be. There's enough food here to feed an army."

Naomi soaked the thick cakes in syrup, and for the next several minutes, she became absorbed in reducing the formidable meal to a few soggy crumbs. Mo did the same to her burger and yanks.

She waited until Naomi ran the last forkful of cake through the syrup before she asked, "Did you find out anything interesting about Father O'Bannon?"

Naomi forked the cake into her mouth and chewed, then took a sip of water. "Joey showed me how to find him in the morgue," she said.

Mo smiled. Joey must be one of the last journalists in America to use that term for a newspaper's computer database of old stories. Naomi plopped her notebook on the table next to her platter and flipped open the cover. She frowned at her thumb, stuck it in her mouth to suck off stray syrup, then paged through a dense thicket of scribbles and doodles.

"You already had most of it in your story," she said, squinting at her notes. "But there was one thing…"

Naomi flipped through several more pages.

"Yeah. Here. Father Eagleston. He was the assistant priest at St. Anne's."

"Yeah. I ran across that name, too. When the bishop transferred him, St. Anne's didn't get a replacement."

"The bishop didn't transfer him."

"He didn't?"

"Nuh-uh. The story about his leaving just said he was going on 'indefinite leave of absence.' Joey said that's what they say when a priest gets busted."

"Busted for what?"

Naomi shrugged. "He didn't know. He said Father Eagleston musta been an alcoholic or a pervert. He said they used to send them all down to New Mexico."

"Did you find any other stories about Father Eagleston?"

"Nuh-uh. There was nothing about him in the paper after that. Joey said whatever he'd done, the diocese covered it up." Naomi flipped her notepad shut. "Do you think it had anything to do with Father O'Bannon getting, you know, killed?"

"I don't know, Naomi. But I know this. You did great work today."

Naomi allowed herself a small smile. "You gonna tell Mrs. Manley?"

"You bet I am."

"I looked up Stanley Bickens on the computer, too."

"Yeah? What did you find out?"

"He got fired a lot."

Mo laughed. "I don't wonder."

Naomi returned to her customary silence all the way back to Mitchell. Mo found herself trying to figure out some possible connection between the banishment of an associate pastor more than a decade ago and the murder of Father O'Bannon.

11

"They just don't sound like chickens!" Gwen Holly Simpkins lamented, putting both hands to her head as if trying
to squeeze out the poor clucking.

"I know," Mo said. "I'm just not sure what to do about it."

Polly Schmeiling, Jeannie Krueger, Tiffany Schuster,
and Suzanne Cheever were having a difficult time getting
into their big number. It was a potential showstopper, Gwen
Holly had assured them, if performed properly.

"It's a delicious song!" she insisted.

Suzanne Cheever glared at her. "It's a stupid song."

"Totally lame," Tiffany added.

"It's supposed to be lame," Mo said. "That's the point.
And the more you camp it up, the better it will go over."

"Yes!" Gwen Holly said. "You have to throw yourselves
into it!"

This earned four sets of eye rolls, but Mo pressed on.
"You have to let yourselves go. If you don't, you'll look lame,
and the song won't work."

"You have to be chickens," Gwen Holly said, "pecking
and cheeping!"

The barbershop quartet, comprised of the Bulldogs'

middle linebacker, the defensive safety, the tight end, and the quarterback, were practicing their big number, "Sincere," twenty feet away, stage left. The flat bass of the tight end and the falsetto tenor of the quarterback were burying the baritone of the middle linebacker. The safety didn't appear to be singing at all. As the four battled their way through the song, Gwen Holly again gripped her head.

"Keep working with them," she said to Mo. "I've got to go help the boys."

Gwen Holly Simpkins bustled off, creating her customary wake.

Mo eyed her charges. They looked exhausted. "Let's take five," she said.

They flopped down on the stage in a rough circle.

"We're working you awfully hard," Mo said. "The idea's supposed to be to have fun."

Polly leaned over and said something to Tiffany, who snorted, putting a hand to her mouth.

"Can you share it?" Mo asked. "We could all use a laugh."

Polly blushed.

"She said," Tiffany volunteered, glancing quickly over her shoulder, "at least Gwen Holly didn't tell us all about the time she played the mayor's wife off–Broadway!"

"For once," Polly said, still blushing.

Mo had to smile. She'd heard the story, too, twice, and she'd only been helping out with the play for a week and a half. "You don't like this play, do you?" she asked.

"She's just mad because she didn't get to be Marian," Tiffany said, pointing at Suzanne.

"I am not!" Suzanne said.

"You shoulda got it," Jeannie said. "You're much better than Brianna."

"Brianna's stuck up," Polly said.

"Remember, ladies," Tiffany said, her voice a reasonable imitation of Gwen Holly's contralto, "there are no small roles. Only small actors!"

Mo laughed.

"She only wanted to be ñ because Jeremy got Harold Hill," Tiffany said.

Suzanne slugged Tiffany on the arm. Mo could tell it hurt.

"Shrew," Tiffany said.

"Bitch," Suzanne said.

"O-kay," Mo said. "Now that we're all relaxed and rested…"

Tiffany glowered at Suzanne, who gazed out over the nonexistent audience.

"We were supposed to do *Jesus Christ, Superstar*," Jeannie said. "That's a cool play!"

The others, except Tiffany, nodded.

"What happened?"

"Some parents said it was sacrilegious," Suzanne said. "They went to Father O…"

"And Father O went to the school board," Polly finished.

"It was goodbye J.C., hello Harold Hill," Jeannie said.

"And we wind up having to be chickens."

Mo laughed.

"Here comes Coach Jensen," Suzanne said.

Mo turned to see the young basketball coach heading their way.

"He probably wants to chew us out for scuffing his precious gym floor," Polly said.

"I'll head him off," Mo said, getting to her feet. "You guys go through your chicken number one more time. And no hitting, please."

Rob Jensen had already reached the stage. He was young, energetic, friendly and, in the words he often used to tell his team what he expected of them, "full of hustle."

"How'd you get roped into this?" he asked, grinning up at Mo.

She shook her head. "I let it slip to Esther Manley that I had done some amateur theater. Gwen Holly was within earshot."

"Ooooh. Major mistake. How are rehearsals coming?"

"At this point, it looks like there's no possible way we'll have this thing pulled together by opening night." Seeing his face cloud with concern, she added, "That's par for the course. It's always chaos up to and including the dress rehearsal."

Rob's face got serious, and Mo couldn't help but think he looked like a little boy about to confess that he'd pilfered a macaroon from the cookie jar.

"I wanted to apologize for making you folks wait until so late to start your rehearsals," he said. "I know how inconvenient it must be. But I can't start basketball practice until Jimmy Fennerty and Jason Vardick can get home, help with the afternoon milking, and get back again."

"It's not your fault. Maybe next time we have a referendum to build a separate auditorium, the voters will be a little kinder."

"Wouldn't that be nice? Well, I'd better scoot. Again, my apologies."

"That's okay. And thanks."

She watched the young coach jog across the gym floor and disappear through the locker room door. She turned back to the problem at hand: trying to get Polly, Jeannie, Tiffany, and Suzanne to cheep and peck their way to stardom.

†††

It was nearly midnight by the time she drove up the long, curving driveway and nosed the little del Sol in next to Doug's SUV at the side of the house. She was surprised to see the living room lights still on, and when she got inside, found Doug standing in front of the floor-to-ceiling bookshelves he'd installed on each side of the fireplace.

"They're finished!" she said. "They look wonderful!"

"Thank you, ma'am." He reached out and pulled her close to him.

"Can we start putting the books in?"

"Tomorrow. I want to give the paint a night to dry."

"They're so nice! You're so nice!" Her arm circled his waist, and she hugged him.

"I just wish it could have been a surprise. But it's kind of hard to cover it up when you're building bookshelves in the living room."

"It'll be a surprise every time I walk into the room."

Side by side, they surveyed the wonder of the bookshelves a long moment.

"How about a nightcap?" she asked.

They walked into the kitchen. Mo got herself a Diet Coke, and Doug filled the kettle at the tap and put it on for tea.

"How's the play coming?" he asked when they were seated at the kitchen table, covered by heaps of magazines, catalogs, and unopened mail.

Mo heaved a sigh. "Gwen Holly always seems to be on the verge of having a stroke, but somehow she manages to keep everything and everyone moving. We should have some kind of show ready."

"As long as you trot their kids out on stage, the parents will be happy."

"I hope so."

"You're later than usual."

"I talked with Naomi Thundercloud after rehearsals."

"Don't tell me she's in the play."

"No, she was in the journalism room. She's spending an awful lot of time there."

"Hard worker."

"And a good one. I'm already wondering how I'll get along without her when her internship is up."

Mo took a long swig of her Diet Coke. Purring softly, Jackie twined Mo's ankles. She bent down and, with a grunt, hoisted the cat into her lap, where he squirmed for a moment, then flopped down.

"Naomi wants to work for the Native paper up north."

"Good for her."

Doug went to the counter to pour his tea. Mo sorted through the most recent layer of mail, tossing unopened envelopes to the floor.

"She said she wants to do a profile on Boomer Bickens for the *Bulldog Beat*."

"Who?"

"You know, 'Stan the Man'."

"You're kidding. That gas bag on the radio?"

"She says a lot of the kids listen to him."

"God help us."

"She thinks he's funny. Actually, I think interviewing him would be good for her. If she wants to be a journalist, she's going to have to learn how to talk to all kinds of people."

"What kind of people is that lunatic? I'm surprised you'd let her in the same room with him."

"He's probably a complete wimp with a big radio voice."

"Hmmm. If you're going to be up a while longer, I'll check my email."

"Sure."

After Doug went into his office, Mo returned to the living room and pulled Father O's books from the carton. She stacked them carefully in front of the new bookshelves, arranging them by fiction and nonfiction.

She peeled the tissue paper away from an old Bible, its soft black covers well worn from much use. She let the Bible fall open to Matthew 5, the teaching known as the Beatitudes. "How blest are the poor in spirit," she read, "the reign of God is theirs."

How often Father O'Bannon must have read these words. How they must have touched him. He had tried to live his life by them.

"Blest too the peacemakers; they shall be called sons of God. Blest are those persecuted for holiness' sake; the reign of God is theirs."

The phone in Doug's office rang. "Stennett," she heard him say, his business phone greeting. She went to the kitchen to throw out the Diet Coke can. Jackie followed her, gathered himself, and jumped up on the counter.

"You've got perfectly good water in your bowl, young man," she said, but then she turned on a trickle of cold water so he could lean over the sink and lap at it.

Doug reappeared in the doorway. "That was Steve Everson. There's a fire at Mansfield Park."

12

"It looks bad," Steve Everson said, shaking his head, "but I don't think there's any structural damage."

They were standing at the foot of the bleachers on the first-base side, near the center grandstand. Yellow crime-scene tape stretched across the stairs leading up into the stands, and a deputy sifted through the debris under the seats. Two dozen rows of wooden benches had been burned out, and several more rows beyond that were charred, but firefighters, alerted by the security guard, had kept the blaze from spreading.

"We'll have to tear out this whole section. Hell, the city should have replaced these seats years ago anyway."

The morning sun had just cleared the home team club-house. Light streamed through the opening between the grandstand and the third-base bleachers.

"Maybe we can convince the insurance clown that the whole grandstand needs to be replaced, huh?" Steve said to Doug.

"I think the insurance clown's right over there," Mo said, and the two men turned to see an improbably tall, cadaverously thin young man climbing up into the center grandstand, his back to them. As they watched, he bent over and peered at one of the seats.

"The fire was over here, Sherlock," Steve muttered. "Hey!" he called out, shading his eyes with his hand.

The man stood, turned and waved. He had large, round glasses that, even from a distance, made his eyes appear enormous and gave him a look of perpetual surprise. He wore a white, short-sleeved dress shirt, open at the neck, and tan slacks. His brown hair fell in waves over each ear. He held a clipboard.

"Just one moment," he called, sounding delighted to see them. He turned and bent down again.

"Now that's one queer duck," Steve said.

The deputy stood up under the bleachers, hitting his head on one of the metal support bars. "Shit," he said, and then added, "'scuse me."

"Did you find something?" Mo asked.

"Naw. Back spasm. I gotta remember to squat instead of bend."

"Words to live by," Steve said.

"How's that?"

"Nothing. Squat, don't bend."

The thin man made his way down out of the grandstand, his legs unfolding to take each stair. He looked as if he might topple over in a strong breeze. As he approached, Mo noted the camera strap slung over his shoulder.

"Hello." He smiled broadly, hand extended. "Fletcher Costram. Pleased to meet you."

"Steve Everson. This is my CFO, Douglas Stennett."

Doug stepped forward and shook the man's hand. Fletcher Costram looked over at Mo.

"Mo Quinn," she said, taking his hand. "I'm just along for the ride."

"You new? I don't believe I've worked with you before," Steve said to Costram.

"New to the area, but not to the company. I worked for them out in Omaha for six—no, make that seven years."

"Ah, beautiful Omaha. Don't know how you could stand to leave."

"It wasn't easy, believe me. Born and raised there. But when opportunity knocks, you got to throw open that door and let him on in. Isn't that about right?"

"Oh, absolutely," Steve said.

Mo heard a car pull into the parking lot beyond the leftfield fence. Lashandra Cooper walked through the open gate and disappeared behind the third-base side bleachers, heading toward them.

Mo walked over, and they met in front of the grandstand. "I didn't expect to see you here," Mo said. "You don't think there's a connection between this fire and Father O's murder, do you?"

"I can't imagine what it could be, but you can't..."

"I know. You can't rule anything out."

"Right. I'm going to take a look around. Haskins here yet?"

"The deputy with the back spasms?"

"That's him. It's his case."

"He's under the bleachers."

"He loves to get dirty."

Fletcher Costram was taking pictures, shooting from field level up into the burned-out section of bleachers. Doug and Steve sat several sections farther down the first-base line, Steve talking while Doug listened and nodded. Deputy Haskins stood in the stands, surveying the damage. Lashandra brushed aside the crime-scene tape and walked towards him. Mo followed.

"They've already dusted for prints," Haskins said as they approached.

Lashandra bent down, her nose almost touching the charred remains of one of the rows, and sniffed. "Lighter fluid. Like you use for the barbecue. That must have been the accelerant."

"We think somebody dragged that garbage can underneath there and started a fire in it. Must have got a pretty good blaze going to make it hot enough to ignite the wood," said Haskins.

Lashandra tapped on the intact portion of bleacher and peeled up several splinters. "It's awfully old and awfully dry. I guess it went up pretty easily."

Mo took her digital camera out of her purse and snapped pictures of the burned-out area, thinking she might use one in the *Doings*.

"Excuse me. Didn't mean to sneak up on you. Fletcher Costram." He held his bony hand out for Lashandra.

"Detective Lashandra Cooper, Dane County Sheriff's Department." She nodded her head, introducing Mo and Haskins.

"Mighty pleased to meet you. I'm getting some pictures for the insurance. I found this." He dug a hand into his shirt pocket. "Over there." He nodded toward the center grandstand. "I was wondering if it might have something to do with the fire."

The sun glinted off his glasses, so that his whole face seemed to glow.

Deputy Haskins turned from gazing at the damage. "Ill take that."

He held his hand out, reaching past Lashandra, and Fletcher Costram poured shreds of paper onto his palm.

"I found this, too."

Again the long, bony fingers probed the shirt pocket,

emerging with the outer wrapper from a roll of wint-o-green LifeSavers. The wrapper had been folded in half once each way, the creases on the folds crisp and new.

"It was just like this when I found it," Fletcher Costram said.

"Where'd you say you found this?" Lashandra asked.

"Over there." He pointed back toward the center grandstand. "Seven rows up, center section. I thought maybe whoever set the fire might have sat over there and watched for awhile. Maybe to make sure it got going good."

"Did you find anything else?" asked Haskins.

"Uh-huh. Yeah."

A third time the fingers dug into the pocket. "I think it's cereal," he said. "You know, like you eat for breakfast."

"Hang on. Lemme get a baggie." Haskins dug in his pocket for a small evidence bag and dumped in Costram's findings. "Is that it?" he asked.

"Yep. Do you think it'll help you catch who did it?"

"You never know, Mr. Costram," said Lashandra. "You're a very observant fellow. Most folks would have missed these."

He ducked his head, and Mo was pretty sure he blushed. "I guess I'm about done here," he said.

Haskins dug into his own shirt pocket and extracted a card, which he handed to Fletcher Costram. "If you think of anything else, please give me a call.

"I sure will do that."

"What do you think?" Lashandra asked Haskins as Fletcher Costram ambled off, all elbows and angles. She indicated the bag of material he had just collected.

"Not a clue," Haskins said.

Mo lowered her camera and looked at the bag. "Paper scut. The stuff you have left when you tear a page out of a spiral notebook."

Lashandra shook her head, and Haskins stuffed the baggie into his pocket.

†††

"They must have been humoring the Stork, right?" Doug asked when Mo told him about the finds on the drive back to Mitchell. "What possible use could any of that junk be?"

"The wrapper was so carefully folded and creased. Who unwraps candy that way?"

"That's the way you unwrap presents."

"That's different. You can save the wrapping paper to use again."

"You having some sort of intuition, Nancy Drew?"

"Not really. Lashandra keeps saying not to rule anything out. Does Steve have a theory about who might have set the fire?"

"No nouns, but a lot of adjectives. He is not a happy camper."

"Insurance will cover it, though, won't it?"

"Should. You don't know for sure until you get the check. Actually, that's not what we were talking about most of the time, though."

"What, then?"

"Believe it or not, we were discussing the war. Turns out he's a peacenik. Not like you and the late Father, but he thinks we made a serious blunder getting involved in Iraq."

"Isn't that an unpopular position for a businessman to take?"

"He keeps a low profile. He's involved in a couple of Internet discussion groups, and he uses a screen name."

"Was he okay with you disagreeing with him?"

"Seemed to be. Mostly I pressed him on what he thought our alternatives were."

"What did he say?"

"Didn't really have any. Do nothing, I guess. You still going to that Latin Mass this afternoon, to make up for missing this morning?"

"Of course."

"You Catholics sure are compulsive about that stuff."

"I don't go because I have to, Doug. I go because I want to."

"If you say so."

"You don't have to come."

"No, no. I want to. Maybe I'll earn a few Brownie points, eh? Besides, it might be a good show."

"Mass isn't a performance for you to critique."

"I'd never accuse it of being entertaining. Hey, come on, I'm kidding. I thought you wanted to convert me."

Mo glared at him, then turned her eyes back to the road. The back of her neck was hot, and her heart was pounding. Saying nothing seemed to be her best bet until she cooled off.

Doug tuned in to his public radio station, and they listened to classical music.

"Everson's divorced," Doug said when they were well beyond Sun Prairie on the county highway. "For all his bluster, I think he's lonely." When Mo remained silent, he added, "I invited him to dinner next Saturday. I hope that's all right. I'll cook."

"You never invite people over!" Mo said with a surprised smile.

"I didn't think you'd mind."

"I don't. Actually, I'm glad for a chance to get to know him."

"By the time you get done interviewing him, you'll have his life story."

"I don't interview our guests."

"Honey, you interview everybody."

She wondered if the fire at Mansfield Park might somehow be connected to Father O's murder. Perhaps Steve Everson would have some insights that would help her either connect the two events or let the idea go.

13

"*Confiteor Deo, omnipotenti et vobis,*" Father Kleinsorge chanted from his makeshift altar in front of the fireplace.

The dozen or so standing with Mo and Doug in the Ortegas' small living room responded, "*Fratres, quia peccavi nimis cogitatione, verbo, opere et emossione.*"

They struck their breasts as they intoned "*mea culpa, mea culpa, mea maxima culpa.*"

"They really say that?" Doug whispered, his lips brushing her ear. "I thought that was a joke."

The gray-haired woman fingering her beads next to Mo glared at them.

"*Kyrie, eleison,*" Father Kleinsorge intoned.

"*Kyrie eleison,*" Mo repeated with the others.

"*Christe, eleison.*"

"*Christe, eleison.*"

"*Kyrie, eleison.*"

"*Kyrie, eleison.*"

Mo made the sign of the cross, index and middle fingers brushing her forehead, passing over her face, and sweeping from left shoulder to right. She felt Doug's eyes on her and tried to concentrate on the ancient Latin rite.

They sat for the first and second readings. As she listened, Mo scanned the room. She recognized no one in the little congregation. That surprised her. Even in a town as small as Mitchell, she couldn't have met everyone, of course, but she had thought she'd encounter at least one familiar face.

They stood while Father Kleinsorge read the Gospel.

"The Gospel of our Lord," he concluded in his rich baritone, rolling out each word as if in a separate padded container.

"Praise to you, Lord Jesus Christ," they intoned in response.

"Please be seated," he said, then waited for them to settle. "I am Father Harvard Kleinsorge. It is my honor and privilege and a rich spiritual blessing to celebrate these sacred mysteries with you this afternoon. I am, of course, deeply saddened and troubled, as are all of you, by the circumstances that have brought me here. As some of you may know, Father Michael O'Bannon and I were dear friends.

"He was an extraordinary man, a man of great conviction and compassion, a quiet warrior for the Gospel. He would have gladly laid down his life for his faith, and now it appears that he has."

There was a stirring among the celebrants.

"We, of course, don't know the circumstances of his untimely death. We may never know. But we do know this. Father Michael O'Bannon was a good and loving man."

Heads nodded. Someone blew loudly into a handkerchief.

Kleinsorge's voice soared up out of its melodious singsong. "We must continue to pray without ceasing, dear ones! We must open ourselves to the power of the Holy Spirit, so that we may help speed the coming of God's Kingdom on earth.

"In the name of the Father," he said, beginning to cross himself, "and the Son, and the Holy Spirit."

With that he sat down, facing them, his expression stern. They sat in heavy silence until he stood to begin the liturgy of the Eucharist.

When the Mass was over and they had received Father's final blessing, Mo put a hand on Doug's arm to keep him from bolting out the door and waited for a few of the other celebrants to speak with Father.

"Ms. Quinn," Father greeted her. "I didn't know you celebrated the Tridentine Mass."

"My first time. Father Kleinsorge, this is my husband, Douglas Stennett."

"Very pleased to meet you, Mr. Stennett."

"Thank you, Father." Doug took the priest's hand. "I'm not Catholic."

"I noticed. What did you think of the service?"

"Quite a workout. Reminded me of a story my grandfather told. You might like it."

"Doug," Mo hissed.

Father Kleinsorge raised an eyebrow. "Do tell," he said.

"It seems a lovely young Catholic lass fell in love with a young man not of the faith." Doug was already grinning in anticipation. "She convinced him to attend Mass with her, but he agreed only on the condition that she tell him exactly what he needed to do, so he wouldn't feel foolish."

A middle-aged man and woman approached and stood to Father Kleinsorge's left. The woman smiled and nodded. The man looked on impassively.

"Well, the priest started the service, and, as good as her word, the young lass kept her boyfriend apprised of exactly what he should be doing. 'Now stand up,' she'd say, and 'Now sit down' and 'Now kneel.' The fellow gamely followed her directions.

"It being quite a hot day, he soon worked up a good sweat, so he took out his handkerchief and swabbed his brow. Then, figuring he'd need the hankie again, he dropped it in his lap instead of putting it back in his pocket.

"Well, our fair lady caught a glimpse of white in his lap out of the corner of her eye. Horrified, she leaned over and hissed, 'Is your fly open?'

"'No,' her young man hissed back. 'Should it be?'"

Doug grinned, looking from Father Kleinsorge to the couple next to him.

Father Kleinsorge frowned, then nodded. "Yes," he said. "I see." He reached out an arm to include the couple in the conversation. "I don't know if you good people have met. Ms. Quinn, Mr. Stennett. These are our hosts, the Ortegas."

The man took a step forward, hand extended. "Juan Ortega. You are most welcome in our home. This is my wife, Olivia."

"Very pleased to meet you," Doug said. "How would you say that in Spanish?"

"*Con mucho gusto,*" Juan said without smiling.

"I'd best pack up and head back to Madison," Father Kleinsorge said. "So nice seeing you again, Ms. Quinn. Nice meeting you, Mr. Stennett. I shall remember that story."

Doug beamed. "Feel free to use it in a sermon."

"You are new to the area?" Olivia Ortega asked Mo.

"We moved here from Chicago almost a year ago."

"She is the one who edits the newspaper in Mitchell," Juan said.

Olivia's eyes widened. "Yes, yes! Of course!" she said. "The one who found the murderer of the man who owned the café!"

"We enjoyed the service," Mo said. "Thank you so much for including us."

"It is your first time?" Juan asked.

"Yes. I didn't know we had a Latin Mass in the area until recently."

"We do not advertise. Those who seek the Latin Mass will find it."

"It is not for everyone," his wife said.

"I bet." Doug said.

"Some come once, out of curiosity, and do not return," Olivia said.

"I think they come expecting us to sacrifice a lamb on the altar," Juan said.

"That's only for special occasions, right?" Doug asked. "Easter and Christmas?"

Juan frowned.

"You knew Father O'Bannon?" Olivia asked Mo.

"Yes. I attend St. Anne's."

"So sad." Olivia shook her head.

"A savage act," Juan said. "Surely the work of the evil one."

"I can't imagine why anyone would do such a thing," Olivia added.

"We talked to that detective," Juan said. "I'm afraid we couldn't be of much help."

"Surely no one in our congregation..." Olivia left the sentence unfinished.

"No," Mo said. "Of course not."

"A few were very upset with Father," Juan said. "They felt that he did not stand up to the new bishop to fight for the Mass. I myself felt that way."

"He told this to the detective," Olivia said.

Juan shrugged. "The police must examine every aspect.

I understand this. You are perhaps examining every aspect, too."

"I'm writing a story about Father O'Bannon. I leave the police work to the police."

"This is best," Juan Ortega said. "This is definitely best."

They talked a few minutes more, and then Mo and Doug took their leave.

"That stuff makes even less sense in Latin," Doug said as they walked down the Ortega's gravel driveway.

He used the device on the key chain to unlock the doors of his SUV. They got in and buckled up. Doug started the car and drove them slowly along the small country lane to the highway.

"That Ortega guy sure is a sourball," he said. "I don't think he even got my joke."

"Maybe he just didn't think it was funny."

"I probably should have told it in Latin, huh? Or Spanish?"

"I'm sure that would have made all the difference."

Doug glanced at her. "You mad at me?"

"No."

"I didn't embarrass you?"

"No more than usual." She smiled at him, and he smiled back.

"Glad to hear it. Also glad to hear you're leaving the police work to the police. No more sleuthing, right?"

"Absolutely. No more sleuthing."

And yet, Mo realized as they headed for home, she couldn't help feeling she was getting closer to a killer.

"It's 'Anything Can Happen Day' here on the Boomer Bickens Radio Program, boys and girls. That's right, friends. It's open season Friday! Any topic you want to talk about. Just be damn sure you've got something to say!

"Want to talk about the street repair insanity in the Mad City? How about trying to defend the governor's idiot veto of the property tax freeze? Go for it! Somebody want to try to support those bleeding heart anti-war pukes who think we should tuck our tails between our legs and leave the people of Iraq to fend for themselves? Rotsa ruck, babies, because I, Stan the Man Bickens, the Boomer man, the voice of reason in a world gone mad, will bury you with the sheer force of my intellect and the fundamental soundness of my arguments.

"So bring it on, babies. We've got two lines open, and I am ready to rumble this morning. But first, we have to pay a few bills. Don't you dare touch that dial, or I'll move into your neighborhood and lower your property values!"

Stan the Man Bickens pushed the headphones back off his ears. He pivoted in his chair to face them and reached for the water bottle by the microphone. Sweat streamed off his face. He took a long swig of water, leaned back, scratched at his ample belly, belched, and laced his fingers behind his head.

"So," he said, looking from Mo to Naomi, "you want to know how I got my start in this wretched business, right?"

Naomi nodded, looking down at the notebook in her lap.

Off the air, Stan the Man's voice went up an octave. Neither on nor off-air voice matched the obese, pasty-faced, middle-aged man. Mo wasn't sure what she had expected, but this surely wasn't it.

"My story's a real tearjerker, believe me." He winked at Mo. "You'll think I'm making it up. Maybe I will be." Bickens laughed. "Nope. All true, all true. I was an orphan. Grew up in a series of foster homes in the beautiful Coon Valley, hard on the Kickapoo River.

"Definitely what you'd call an 'at risk' child. I'm sure I had ADD and all that other alphabet crappola, too. Thank God Ritalin hadn't been invented yet.

"I listened to the radio all the time. Radio was my storyteller. I guess it was the one thing that stayed the same, no matter where I went. I'd sit on my bed sometimes and pretend I was an announcer. You ever do anything like that? I'd use one of those tubes the toilet paper comes on for a microphone. I'd do whole shows, all the voices. I'd do the news, sports and weather out of the newspaper, make stuff up, try out a few one-liners, everything except the music."

Bickens leaned forward, waiting for Naomi's hand to stop moving across her notepad. "I knew I was starting to get good the night my foster mother banged on the door and told me to turn the radio down. And the radio wasn't even on. It was me."

He leaned back, the chair groaning under his bulk. He glanced at the clock, jerked the headphones back over his ears, and pivoted to the microphone. "We'll get to your phone rants in just a minute," he said. "But first, have you been to Rocky's Sports Bar lately? Oh, sure, you've gone out there to catch a snootful. But have you tried Rocky's lunch specials?" His voice dipped to a low, confidential purr. "Friends, the food at Rocky's is absolutely top notch, and the prices are incredibly reasonable.

"No paying seven bucks for a plate full of sprouts and grass at Rocky's, folks. For under five bucks, you can get yourself a real burger. I'm talking a half-pound of prime Angus beef, here, friends.

"And you can smoke your little lungs out at Rocky's!"

While Boomer enthused about his friend Rocky and all the fine folks who work with him to make sure you feel right at home, Mo watched Naomi scramble to catch up with her notes. This was ideal for a beginning interviewer— a minute or two of interview at a time, punctuated by frequent breaks.

"Jack! You're on the Boomer Bickens Program. What's up, my man?"

"Boomer, you're the best, man. I listen to you every day."

"You need a life, Jack. What's up?"

"I wanna talk about the university's supposed crackdown on students' binge drinking."

"Supposed? You don't think the chancellor is sincere about wanting area bars to stop giving students drink specials?"

"Yeah. That's my..."

"So the U can continue to sell beer to them without competition! Oh, the hypocrisy! We don't want students drinking too much beer—unless we sell it to them! Give-me-a-break!

"We got Harley Harvey from Mt. Horeb on the line! What's shakin', Double H?"

The little studio was awash in newspapers, scraps of wire copy, and empty water bottles. A thermos and a pair of scuffed slippers nestled on the floor by Stanley's feet. Mo wondered what Naomi was making of it all—and what sort of profile she'd write. She thought of her own first attempts at interviewing, how nervous she'd been. Peoples' kindness and good humor, plus their eagerness to talk about their passions, had gotten her through, but it had taken a while.

"You are putting me on!" Boomer screamed into the microphone suspended in front of him. "You are freakin' putting me on, Weasel! I'm soft on the war? I'm support- ing terrorism?" Bickens balled his fists and pounded them on the table on both sides of his computer keyboard. His water bottle jumped and landed at his feet. "Just how did you manage to come to a conclusion like that?"

"It's easy. You…"

"This is all about my not kissing George W's hairy little Texas hiney, isn't it? If you aren't one hundred percent behind the Prez, you're a traitor, right? Well, let me tell you something, buddy boy. It's the President who's selling out this country, okay? You hearing this, Weasel? He and his gang of oil thieves. You want to pin the treason tail on anybody, buddy, you'd better start at the White House."

"Bickens, you've got your head so far…"

"I'd say you were a complete idiot, but you've obviously got a few parts missing. You're a moron. You're a joke."

He stabbed at the console until he hit the button he wanted. "I gotta play a couple more commercials here," he said. "If anybody else out there wants to say anything nice about that little Texas phony, I'll be happy to tell you how incredibly screwed up you are right after the break."

Bickens turned to face them, smiling. "That guy calls

about ten times a week." He leaned forward and put his pudgy hands on his knees. "So, where were we?"

Naomi leafed back through her notes, but Bickens charged ahead. "When I turned eighteen, living in my umpteenth foster home, I decided it's time to make my mark in the world. So I split. You bet I did. I hit the road. That old witch Myra Kessels probably didn't even know I'd gone until the support checks stopped showing up."

With Naomi scribbling, Stanley Bickens recounted how he hitchhiked to Richland Center and got his first job in radio. "I opened up in the morning, turned the transmitter on, rewrote wire copy, swept the place out, anything that needed doing.

"Blaine Arthur. That was the name of the old sot who had the morning show. At least, that's what he was calling himself then. He'd drunk his way out of jobs all the way across the country, each time dropping down a rung. I don't know where you drop after Richland Center, but I'll bet it ain't pretty.

"Anyway, it wasn't long before I was writing all his copy for him. Sometimes he'd be so hung over, he couldn't even work the board, so I started doing that for him, too. They didn't have an engineer. I did everything—even filled in on air for a minute or two sometimes when Blaine was in the can."

Naomi glanced at the clock; Boomer noticed.

"Don't worry. We went right into the national news feed, and Keith's supposed to get his ass in here and do the local news in…" He eyed the clock. "Twenty-two seconds. Let's see how close he cuts it.

"Anyway, I was living in a room over a bar that I got for nothing for sweeping the dump out before work. I was getting up at 3:30, never needed an alarm clock, still don't. So, I wake up one morning, and it's snowing like a son-of-a-bitch, and the plow isn't even getting through. Nothing's moving."

The door of the booth flew open, cracking Naomi's chair broadside, and a man even fatter than Stanley Bickens charged in.

"Are you boring these poor ladies with your bullshit? Don't believe a word of it, sweethearts. Stick around, and I'll tell you the real story. I'll even give you a copy of his rap sheet."

The man leaned over Naomi, grabbed the microphone, and swung it toward him on its long arm. He clutched several copy sheets.

"I'm Keith Manning, and this is your seven a.m. local news report, brought to you by Duke's Auto Repair, serving the Capital City for over forty years. You can trust your car to The Duke.

"At this hour, we're keeping an eye on a breaking story for you. Fireman have responded to a three-alarmer at the recycling center on South Park Street."

"I figured I'd best get my ass to work, snow or no snow," Stanley said, leaning toward Mo and Naomi and lowering his voice only slightly while Keith Manning delivered his news report. "So I wrapped up in every piece of clothing I owned and started walking."

A large V of sweat began at Manning's waist and tapered down his broad backside. Mo could see little else.

"The snow literally drifted up to my waist in places, and my eyelids kept freezing shut. But I was young and dumb and figured the station and its two-dozen listeners were counting on me, so I kept going.

"I opened the joint up and warmed up the transmitter, like always. We always started off with a network feed, and I managed to get that on the air okay. But then it's almost time for the *Blaine Arthur Program*, and still no sign of Blaine Arthur, or a replacement, or the station manager, or anybody else.

"So I pull some wire copy—thank God the teletype's working—open up the mike and start reading. When I get to the weather, I use a different voice and really ham it up. 'Winds twenty five to thirty five miles per hour,' I say, and then whistle into the microphone like I was this big zephyr shooting through the studio. Stupid stuff like that.

"When I run out of wire copy, I just start making stuff up, telling jokes, doing voices, anything I can think of."

"In case you're wondering why the Mouth that Bored is being so uncharacteristically quiet during the newscast," Manning said into the microphone, "he's busy trying desperately to impress two lovely young ladies he has somehow managed to lure into the studio."

Boomer reached up and tore the microphone from the newsman's hands.

"I figured you didn't need any help messing up the news, Manning. You're quite the expert at it."

Keith Manning was already waddling out the door, restoring Mo's view.

"But he's right, babies. I am indeed talking with two lovely women. We have Ms. Monona Quinn, editor of the *Mitchell Doings*, and Ms. Naomi Lighting Fork, a student intern with the newspaper. Naomi is here to interview yours truly for *Playgirl Magazine*. At least that's what she told me when she insisted I do the interview in the nude.

"Tell us, Naomi." He swung around so that his knees almost touched hers. "How would you assess the state of the news media in America today? Overall, I mean. Are they fair and balanced? Or do you detect a slight tilt to the left, perhaps?"

Naomi stiffened and looked around at Mo.

"This is radio, dear. You can't just shrug. You have to use words."

"I dunno," Naomi said, her voice barely a whisper.

"No opinion on media bias, huh? Okay, then, how about the war? Do you agree with our friend Weasel, who again abused our airwaves with his warmongering rant awhile ago? Do you think we should back the President, no matter how many people he kills?"

Boomer pushed the microphone directly in front of Naomi.

"I dunno," she said again.

Boomer waited, leering at her.

"I did have a question, though," Naomi said.

"You've come to the right place! I've got all the answers."

"I was wondering…"

"Yes? What were you wondering, my little Pocahontas?"

"I was wondering about your military record. Did you fight in Vietnam?"

The leer faded. The weight of the dead air now rested squarely on Boomer's sloped shoulders. "I didn't have the privilege of serving in our Armed Forces," he said, his mouth smiling but his eyes glared at Naomi. "My repeated efforts to pass the physical exam failed, due to chronic migraine headaches."

He looks like he's got a migraine coming on right now, Mo thought.

Boomer swung back to face the board. "I see the lines are all lit up, and we'd better give some callers a chance to express themselves. It's Freaky Friday, folks. Anything goes. Pit Bull out in Black Earth! You're sharing the dairy air with the Boomer."

"You dodged the draft, huh?" the voice on the phone

said. "I thought you were at least in the Guard or something."

Boomer glared at Naomi. She didn't notice because she was busy taking notes. Mo tapped her shoulder and nodded toward the door.

"Interview's over," she said as soon as they were out in the hallway. "Your source is through talking to you today."

"Did I mess up?"

"No, you didn't mess up. You did great."

"He's such a jerk." Naomi looked down at her notepad. "How am I going to write about him?"

"Quote him accurately and let the readers decide. It'll be a great piece."

She nodded. "I'm glad you made me do this. It was hard, but it was good."

Mo smiled. "The important stuff usually is."

"Oh, there's nothing half way, about the Iowa way to greet you, if we greet you, which we may not do at all."

Mo watched tensely from the wings as the chorus of would-be small-town Iowans labored to assure Professor Harold Hill that he could eat his fill of all the food he brought himself. When she had performed, she'd never had the actor's classic anxiety dream. But she'd had it last night—on stage, naked, with no idea what her next line was, or even what play she was in. Mo's quartet hadn't managed to get through its 'Pick a Little, Talk a Little' number successfully in rehearsals, not even one time. What were the odds that they'd nail it now?

She leaned forward and peeked around the curtain. The last time she'd looked, the gymnasium had been an ocean of empty metal folding chairs bobbing on a sea of blue tarps to protect Rob Jensen's floor. Now the chairs all held people, an audience, an opening-night full-house.

Mo spotted Doug, looking uncomfortable in coat and tie and wedged between Andy Krueger and Peter Hanson. Mo hadn't insisted, hadn't even suggested he attend. Maybe he was trying to make up for his behavior at the Tridentine

Mass. Or maybe he was just being the nice, supportive guy he usually was.

"Mrs. Quinn?"

Hillary Broderick, the stage manager, looked even more worried than usual. "Mrs. Simpkins needs you right away." She grabbed Mo's arm as if she intended to drag her if Mo didn't come along. "There's something wrong with Jeannie."

"Lead the way," Mo whispered, her heart sinking.

Poor Jeannie. She had a good voice, and she'd be nice looking if she tried, but she was so shy, so sure she'd fail at whatever she did.

Gwen Holly was huddling with Polly, Tiffany and Suzanne, who looked completely out of place in their gingham dresses. The director had wrapped her stocky five-foot frame in black velvet.

"I'm afraid we have a bit of a situation on our hands," Gwen Holly whispered urgently when she spotted Mo. "It's Jeannie. A serious case of opening-night jitters."

"She's puking her guts out," Suzanne said.

"Shhhhh." Gwen Holly hissed. "There is a play going on."

"Where is she? I'll talk to her," Mo whispered.

"I knew she couldn't do it," Polly said. "She's such a little wuss."

"She's in the dressing room," Gwen Holly said.

"I guess we won't be able to do our big chicken number," Suzanne said. "Darn."

Tiffany looked stricken but said nothing.

"The show must go on, my dears," Gwen Holly said.

"How? We can't do the stupid song without Jeannie."

"If Jeannie is unable to perform, perhaps your wonderful mentor would be willing to step in and save the day."

A beat passed before Mo realized she was the "wonderful mentor" Gwen Holly had in mind. Before she could protest, the director broke free and bore down on Harley Cox, the lumbering offensive lineman cast in the key role of the anvil salesman. Poor Harley had pretty much lost his big line– "But he doesn't know the territory"–to a bad attack of dry mouth during the opening train number and was about to hear about it now.

Against the black backdrop, Gwen Holly's pale face seemed to float. Mo watched, mesmerized by the effect.

"So, how about it?" Suzanne asked. "You going to take the puker's place?"

"Oh, I certainly hope not."

Jeannie appeared to be past the throwing-up stage and into serious sobbing when Mo found her slumped over the makeup table. Mo sat next to her and put a hand gently on her heaving shoulder.

"You can't make me go out there!" Jeannie wailed.

Mo stroked the girl's silky brown hair. "No one's going to make you do anything."

"I didn't want to be in this stupid play! It was my mother's idea." Jeannie lifted her head, turning her tear-savaged face toward Mo. "I've ruined everything!"

Mo dug out a handkerchief and gave it to her. Jeannie stabbed at her eyes with it, and the cloth came away streaked with black eye shadow.

"I've never done anything right in my whole life."

"I doubt that very much. But let's just deal with the problem at hand."

"You don't understand. My life is over."

"Life will go on. Trust me."

"I'll bet you never did anything this bad."

"How about falling half out of your dress on stage?"

"Really?"

"I had the lead in *The Bad Seed* my senior year in high

school. I had this big scene with Leroy, who's the only one who suspects how evil I really am. My stupid dress was just velcroed in the front so I could get in and out of it fast. Somehow my sleeve got caught on the velcro, and zip. Leroy got himself an eyeful."

"Oh, my God. What did you DO?"

"What any cool, professional actor would do. Shrieked and ran off stage."

Jeannie put a hand to her mouth, her eyes huge. "Oh, no."

"Oh, yeah. The poor guy playing Leroy–he was a junior named Jason Koch–had to pretend it was all part of the act and fill for about a minute and a half while they got me calmed down and put back together. He must have done a great job, because I could hear the audience laughing and clapping. In fact, the director liked it so much, she wrote it into the next performance. Not the part about the dress, though."

"You must have died. How could you go back out there?"

"I really don't know. I guess I just figured it would be worse not to."

"What happened?"

"I got through it. I was okay as long as I didn't make eye-contact with Jason."

Jeannie blew her nose into Mo's hankie.

"I got a standing ovation at the end of the performance," Mo said. "I was never quite sure what it was for."

Jeannie laughed.

"Okay, kiddo. Decision time. Do you want to give it a shot? Otherwise, you're going to have to help me get into your costume."

"You'd do that?"

"As long as there's no velcro."

Jeannie laughed again, sniffled, dabbed at her eyes. "I must look awful."

"Nothing we can't fix."

Jeannie bit her lip and nodded, and Mo got busy on repairs.

Gwen Holly appeared on the verge of collapse when Mo and Jeannie arrived in the wings just seconds before the quartet was due on stage. Mo gave Jeannie's hand a quick squeeze, and Jeannie squeezed back hard.

As she followed the other three out from the wings, Mo said a silent prayer. She held her breath as they launched into a perfect series of pecks and cheeps. Jeannie stepped out of formation right on cue to deliver her big one-word line–"Balzac!" The football players came in nearly on time and almost on key to blend in their "Good night, ladies" on the final chorus. And then the River City matrons were heading for the wings, their rears thrust out, their heads pushed forward, their arms flapping–to laughter and wild applause from the audience.

"We were great!" Tiffany announced.

"I guess we didn't stink it up too bad," Polly said.

"I still think the whole thing's gross," Suzanne said.

Jeannie wrapped Mo in a fierce hug. "Oh, thank you!" she said at the same time Mo said, "You were wonderful."

The rest of the play seemed to fly by, and soon the cast took its bows. Jeremy Hodgekiss and Brianna Douglass stepped out, hand in hand, to intensified cheers. Jeremy beckoned a blushing Gwen Holly Simpkins out on stage and presented her with a bouquet of long-stemmed roses.

When the curtain closed, the young actors shrieked, and even the stagehands got in on the kissing and hugging. It was some time before they calmed down enough for Gwen Holly to give them their notes for the Saturday matinee.

By the time Mo got home, it was past midnight, and she was exhausted.

Doug greeted her at the door. "A triumph," he said, kissing her.

"Really?"

"Yeah. The audience ate it up. Even the ones who didn't have kids in the play loved it. And your hens really came through."

"I was so proud of them. Especially Jeannie. We almost lost her."

The phone message light was flashing when she went into the kitchen. Mo punched the play button.

"Hey," Lashandra's voice greeted her, "we got the prints back from the ballpark. Nothing that can't wait. Give me a call at home if you want to. I'll be up late."

Lashandra picked up on the first ring.

"Hi. This is Mo."

"Hey, how was the play?"

"Doug says we knocked 'em dead. What's the news?"

"The fingerprints from the ballpark came back from the lab."

"And...?"

"They hardly got anything useable, and none of what they did get matched anybody in the system."

"So. Nothing, huh?"

"Pretty much. A print they took off the railing of the stairs in the center grandstand is a two-point match with the print we got off the knife that killed Father O'Bannon."

"What does that mean, 'two-point'?"

"It means it's inconclusive and probably just a coincidence."

"The same person who killed Father O could have set the fire?"

"It's a remote possibility."

"What possible connection could there be?"

"Probably none. But we should let Steve Everson know anyway, just to be on the safe side. If it is the same guy, and I don't think it is, but if it is, Everson better be sure somebody's watching his back. He could be next on somebody's list."

"He's coming to my house for dinner. Do you want me to talk to him?"

"Sure. Just don't be overly dramatic about it."

"Do I strike you as the overly dramatic type?"

She was probably overreacting, Mo decided after they had finished their conversation, but that woman still managed to crawl under her skin.

††

By the time she got home from the cast celebration after the Saturday matinee, Doug had the table set and dinner shaping up nicely.

"Steak and potatoes," he said. "Good and also easy to prepare. With dinner rolls and a vegetable stirfry. Do you think we need a salad, too?"

"No. That sounds great. Did you plan anything for dessert?"

"Raspberry sherbet and finger cookies."

"Very nice. Can I help?"

"I think we're in good shape. All we need is the guest of honor."

A harsh rapping at the front door made his eyes open wide. "My gosh, he's early."

"I'll keep him entertained."

As Mo hurried through the living room to get the door, she realized that Doug was nervous about having the boss over for dinner.

"Hi. Come in."

Steve Everson held out a vase filled with an assortment of fresh flowers in reds and yellows.

"Thank you."

He brought his other hand out from behind his back bearing a bottle of red wine from Stag's Leap Vineyards.

"My goodness."

Everson had dressed for the occasion with blue blazer, gray slacks, and blue- and red-striped tie.

"Doug! Mr. Everson's here!"

"Make it 'Steve,' please. If I'd known he was cooking," he said loud enough to be heard in the kitchen, "I would have stopped for a burger on my way."

"You'll be glad you didn't." Doug stuck his head in at the door. "I've slaughtered the fatted calf."

"That would make me the prodigal."

"Let's serve this nice wine with dinner," Mo said, ushering Everson into the kitchen. "Would you like a drink?"

"Only if it's the custom of the house."

"We have been known to take a splash before meals," she said.

"Would you be so kind as to splash a little brown whiskey in a glass with some ice for me?"

"I think I can manage that."

Mo had thought about inviting a woman to even the party out—not as any sort of fix-up for one of Madison's most eligible divorcees, but for someone for her to talk to in case the conversation devolved into business. But to her delight, the talk ranged over current movies and novels, reality TV, and the woeful state of affairs in Washington, D.C.

That last topic led them into a discussion of what Steve called, "our dirty little war of aggression." Having tilted previously at the ballpark, Steve and Doug jumped right into the middle of an argument.

"I suppose you'd just let that madman kill innocent people," Doug said.

"Which madman are you referring to? And no, the fact that I oppose this war does not mean that I support the slaughter of innocents."

"But you would do nothing."

"Dougie, evil dictators are doing unspeakable things all over the globe. We don't go after them."

"One at a time."

"God, what a thought. You seem to assume that we've been ordained policeman to the world. The truth of the matter is, and you know this is true, we've set up half the tinhorn dictators currently ravaging their own countries. Hell, we propped up Saddam, so he could help us hold Iran down."

Mo fought the impulse to join in on Steve's side of the argument. She didn't want Doug to feel she was ganging up on him or being disloyal. Besides, Everson needed no help from her as he reeled off a blistering catalog of events and statistics.

By the time she cleared the plates and served the cookies and sherbet, they had changed the subject anyway.

"Why are folks so upset about the possibility of a highway expansion?" Steve asked. "I'd think it would be a real boon to the local economy."

"That sounds like a safe enough subject," Mo said. "Can I get anyone some decaf?"

"I'd love some," Steve said.

"I'll get it," Doug said.

"Sit. Sit."

"I'm not exactly a neutral bystander in the matter," Steve was telling Doug when Mo came back from the kitchen with the coffeepot, creamer, sugar bowl and three sets of cups and saucers on a tray. "As you'll discover when you get a bit deeper into my finances, I'm an investor in the condo project east of town."

"Really?" Mo set his saucer and cup to his right. She found herself startled by the revelation and couldn't account for the feeling.

"A very small investor, believe me, but I put everything I could scrape together into it. I think it's a marvelous opportunity. A lot of people are fed up with the traffic and crime in Madison. They want a little slice of the simple country life–within easy commuting distance of their employment."

"At the risk of destroying the simple country life they're seeking," Mo noted.

"Growth must be carefully planned," Steve said. "Thank you," he added as she poured his coffee.

"Speaking of crime in the big city," Doug said, "anything new on the fire at the ballpark?"

"You probably know about the fingerprint."

"What fingerprint?" Doug asked, glancing at Mo.

"They lifted a print at the park that's a match for the murderer of Father O'Bannon."

"Really."

"Detective Cooper says it's highly unlikely that they're a match," Mo said.

"That's not what I heard," Steve said.

"Who'd you hear it from?"

"Why didn't you tell me?" Doug asked Mo at almost the same time.

"I hadn't had a chance to. Besides, it's only a two-point match. That apparently barely qualifies as a coincidence."

"Still," Steve said, "if it is the same guy, I could be next on his hit list."

But when Doug expressed his concern, Steve laughed

the notion off. The conversation shifted to other topics, and Steve took his leave after a second cup of decaf.

Mo insisted that Doug relax while she cleaned up in the kitchen. As she submerged the good china in hot, sudsy water, she tried to sort out the feelings their dinner guest had sparked in her. She was now thinking of him, she realized, not only as a potential target for the killer, but as a man with a motive himself for being involved in the killing of Father O.

Both about equally likely, she decided. A two-point "coincidental" match on the fingerprint and a tenuous tie through an investment in a condo development.

Still, the thought nagged at her until the therapeutic powers of hot water and easy physical labor soothed her into a gentler frame of mind.

16

Mo looked up from her computer to see Naomi standing in front of her desk.

"Hi. I didn't hear you come in. Is it five o' clock already?"

Naomi shook her head. "I came early." She extended her hand, offering Mo several crisp sheets of copy paper.

"Your profile?"

Naomi looked at the floor.

"Do you want me to read it now?"

She seemed to have to fight her head to get it to nod. Mo smiled as she took the pages.

"I'll go work on the files," Naomi said.

Mo said a silent prayer that the piece would be good and began to read.

BOOMER BICKENS GETS AROUND
By Naomi Thundercloud
For the Bulldog Beat

If Stanley 'Boomer' Bickens offends you, don't worry. He probably won't be around long.

'Stan the Man' is the morning shock jock for WCCC-FM in Madison. The self-proclaimed "lawsuit waiting to happen" has been on the air locally for six months and is a favorite among Mitchell-Prairie Rapids High students. But his history of losing jobs suggests that he might not be around for six more months.

In the world of radio, 'on-air personalities' (we're not supposed to call them 'disc jockeys' anymore) change jobs more often than Madonna changes her look. Even so, our man Stan seems to have an unusually hard time holding a job.

"I've been around," Mr. Bickens admits. "It's the nature of the business. You come in on Monday morning, and somebody else is sitting in your chair."

His eight-month gig in Winnemucca, Nevada, ended when he told a joke on air that the station manager deemed obscene by local standards. (It's a riddle: 'Why is a woman like a frying pan?' I'm pretty sure my editor would think the answer was obscene, too, and I don't want to lose my internship.)

He lasted almost 18 months in Sandusky, Iowa, before sticking the mike in his mouth again. This time it was his suggestion that listeners dump their garbage on the mayor's lawn during the refuse collectors' strike. Lots of them did, and the mayor was not amused.

Mr. Bickens didn't seem too upset when reminded of the incident. "Screw 'em if they can't take a joke," he said (except that he didn't say 'screw').

Then it was on to Mexico, Missouri, where Mr. Bickens lost his job after only three months when he locked the newscaster in the restroom right before he was due on the air.

"I hated that job anyway," Mr. Bickens said. "It was one of those... 'music for old farts' formats. How many times can you listen to Mood Indigo before you go nuts?"

The phone rang, and Vi picked up. After a brief exchange, she covered the mouthpiece.

"Juan Ortega? You want me to tell him you'll call back?"

"No," Mo said. "I'll take it."

She picked up the receiver and pushed the flashing button. "This is Mo. How are you, Señor Ortega?"

"Very fine, thank you. I hope this isn't a bad time to call."

"Good as any." Mo put Naomi's story on her desk and grabbed her notepad.

"I thought of something after our conversation last Sunday. It's probably not important, but Olivia thought I should call and tell you."

"Go ahead."

"A couple of weeks back, someone came to our little Mass who hadn't been there before. You can't help but notice when there are so few of us."

"Yes?"

"Afterwards, nobody seemed to know him."

"Is that unusual?"

"Yes. Sometimes one of the regulars will invite a friend, but they are usually the only visitors we get."

"I understand."

"It wasn't just that, though. He didn't really seem to know what was going on. Kind of like the fellow in that joke your husband told."

Mo blushed at the memory.

"He did not say a word to anyone the whole time. Afterwards, he waited outside, and when Father O'Bannon left, he followed him to his car. He seemed to be quite upset."

"How so?"

"He seemed to be talking very fast, and he was waving his hands."

"Did you hear any of the conversation?"

"No. I was watching from the window."

"Did you get this fellow's name?"

"No. As I say, he didn't talk to anybody except for Father O'Bannon. He might have signed the guest book. I could check. He was a little man, shorter than me, maybe twenty five or thirty years old. His clothes were messy."

"Anything else stand out about him?"

"During the sermon, he took a notebook out of his backpack and wrote things down. I thought that was strange."

"And he hasn't come back?"

"No. Just that once."

"And this was how long ago?"

"A month. Five weeks, maybe. Do you think it is important?"

"I'm not sure. Did you tell the police about him?"

"No. I didn't think of it. Do you think I should?"

"Yes. I've got the number. Just a sec."

Mo opened the top desk drawer, rummaged around, and pulled out the card she wanted. She read Lashandra Cooper's number to Ortega.

"As I said, Olivia thought I should tell you. I will call that detective and tell her, too."

"Good. Thank you, Señor Ortega."

"I want to do whatever I can."

"We all do."

Mo broke the connection and laid the headset on her desk. Naomi was watching her from her stool in front of the scanner across the room. She looked away quickly. Mo went back to reading the story.

THE MAKING OF A SHOCK JOCK

Mr. Bickens got his start at a small station in Richland Center. He was just 18 when he made his on-air debut, when a snowstorm prevented the regular morning host from getting to the station.

"So I pull some wire copy" off the Associated Press Teletype, Mr. Bickens remembers, "open up the mike and started reading. When I get to the weather, I use a different voice and kind of ham it up.

"When I run out of wire copy, I just start making stuff up, telling jokes, doing voices, anything I can think of."

The station manager heard him on his car radio as he struggled to get through the storm. By the time he got there, he was ready to offer Mr. Bickens a show of his own.

He'd been getting ready for that moment for a long time.

"I'd sit on my bed sometimes and pretend I was an announcer," he recalls. "I'd do whole shows, all the voices. I'd read the news, sports and weather, just making stuff up, try out a few one-liners, everything except the music."

Radio is his passion, he says, "the only thing I know how to do."

"Mo?" Vi called from across the room, hand over mouthpiece. "Lashandra Cooper?"

"Hi. What's up?" Mo said.

"I wondered if you're free later on. I'd like to buy you dinner at that little diner."

"Charlie's closes at 3:00," Mo said, trying to keep the surprise out of her voice.

"You're kidding. They don't serve dinner?"

"Nope. That's life in the small town. They'd roll the sidewalks up at sundown, except we don't have sidewalks."

The detective laughed.

"We could eat at Adamski's Supper Club."

"I pass it on the way into town, right?"

"Right. How about I meet you there?"

"I'll pick you up. I was hoping we could poke around at the school first."

"You have a new lead?"

"Not really. I just keep thinking I missed something out there."

"Okay. When?"

"In an hour?"

"See you then. Oh, hey?"

"Yes?"

"Did you just get a call from Juan Ortega?"

"No. Should I have?"

"He said he'd call right away. I thought that's why you'd called me."

"Nope. No Mr. Ortega."

"That's strange. Well, I'll fill you in when I see you."

"Okay."

Mo read Naomi's story through from the beginning, this time with a pencil in her hand. The final section bore the subtitle:

SOMETIMES HIS CALLERS EVEN SCARE STANLEY

Not surprisingly, given his confrontational style, Mr. Bickens' callers express some rather extreme positions–from belief in the presence of extraterrestrials to the conviction that the Pope is the anti-Christ. They do, that is, until Mr. Bickens cuts them off, which he does when he doesn't agree with them.

Many of the callers are regulars, and none is more regular than one known to listeners as 'Angel.' Angel insists that abortion is murder, a position that causes Stanley to go into a rage.

'You give me the knife, and I'll perform the abortion myself,' he ranted before hanging up on Angel after one especially heated exchange.

Then there's Weasel, Stan the Man's most aggressive opponent. Although Mr. Bickens is a strong supporter of U.S. military intervention in Iraq, Weasel doesn't think he's strong enough. When Mr. Bickens expressed reservations about President Bush's policies recently, Weasel accused him of treason.

Mr. Bickens counterattacked, calling Weasel a "moron" and an "idiot."

"He even scares me sometimes," Mr. Bickens noted off the air.

And what will he do if history repeats itself, and he again finds himself without a job?

"Move on down the line," he says. "Find another microphone and do my thing." #

Mo smiled at the little hatch mark "#" at the end of the story. Only the veterans still used it. The real old-timers used "30." Mo figured Mrs. Manley must have taught Naomi the notation.

She looked up to find Naomi's gaze on her, serious, questioning, from across the room. Mo waved her over.

"It's very good," she said.

Relief spread over Naomi Thundercloud's face like a sunrise.

"You've got some wonderful quotes here, but I don't remember him saying some of these things. The quote about somebody else being in your chair on Monday morning, for example. Where did that come from?"

"I called him up the day after the interview. He told me lots more stuff."

"Very good. How about his job history? Did he give you all that?"

"He told me what stations he'd worked for. I called the newspapers in Winnemucca, Nevada, and Mexico, Missouri, to see if anybody there remembered him and why he'd left the stations. Did I do something wrong?"

"No. You did everything exactly right."

"The story's really okay?"

"Naomi, it's very good. The AP will probably pick it up."

Naomi's eyes got huge.

"That's a good thing. As long as everything you have here is accurate. You've checked and double-checked, right?"

"Uh-huh."

"I need your list of sources."

Naomi dug around in her purse, extracted her notepad, and handed it over. "You can change it any way you want to," Naomi said, her eyes on the floor.

"It doesn't need changing. This is really good work."

The shy smile spread across Naomi's face again. "You're really going to publish it?"

"Of course I'm going to publish it. With your byline. Have you shown this to Mrs. Manley?"

Naomi shook her head. "I wanted to show it to you first. Do you think I should?"

"Oh, yes. I think you should. I think she'll be very pleased."

After Naomi left, Mo returned several phone calls Vi had deemed not crucial enough to interrupt her for, and by the time she got done, Lashandra Cooper was pulling up in front of the *Doings* building.

17

The sun was low in the west, and everything was locked up when Lashandra and Mo got to St. Anne's.

"What are we looking for?" Mo asked as they walked around the building.

"Damned if I know. Little curls of paper? A hunk of cereal? Did I tell you the lab IDed the cereal? Quaker Oats Squares."

Lashandra squatted down to peer into the bushes under the window of the classroom where Father O'Bannon had been murdered. "It hasn't rained since the murder. If the murderer left something behind, it might still be here."

"But they've gone over every inch. And the kids have been running all over the place."

"I know." Lashandra got up, peered around at the broad parking lot/playground, empty now of kids and cars. "What was Father O'Bannon doing in the classroom in the middle of the night?" Lashandra was thinking out loud. "Did he come there on his own, or did the murderer bring him there? There was no sign of forced entry, so Father O'Bannon must have let himself in with a key. Was the murderer here, waiting, when Father got back from dinner, or did he show up later?"

"Could the murderer have had his own key?"

Lashandra frowned. "I thought the priest, the house-keeper, and the custodian had the only keys."

Mo shrugged. "Just not ruling anything out."

Lashandra laughed. "You have been listening."

She walked slowly across the parking lot, shielding her eyes against the sun, and Mo followed.

"If he were waiting," Lashandra muttered, "where would he wait?"

They walked across the concrete to the pine trees separating the schoolyard from an adjoining backyard. Lashandra stopped and squatted down, Mo almost bumping into her.

"Did you find something?"

"They're pretty faint, but these are boot prints."

Mo squatted next to her.

"There's a fairly good print of the heel."

Mo strained to see in the failing light.

"They're awfully small to belong to an adult," Lashandra said. "That rules out the custodian. He's got real gunboats." She fished a Polaroid camera out of her shoulder bag, squatted on her haunches and took several shots. "Whoever made these prints could have been hiding behind the tree."

"It might have been a kid playing hide and seek."

"Do they still do that?"

"The ones who don't have Game Boys, maybe. Hey."

"What?"

"Frankie French wears hiking boots as soon as it gets too cold for Birkenstocks."

Lashandra stood. "We need to get a look at the treads

on his boots. I suppose we could poke around the woods behind his house when he's not around."

"Haven't they already done that?"

"Yeah, but they weren't looking to match up boot prints."

"Wait. We don't need to do that. We can check the town hall. He's out there for every committee meeting."

"The town hall's got a dirt floor?"

"They've been renovating. There's sawdust all over the place. I don't think they ever sweep up."

"It's worth a try."

They took Mo's del Sol and sped out the county road to the dilapidated town hall. When Lashandra tried the door, it was locked.

"We could try a window," Mo said.

"Hold on a minute." Lashandra dug a knife out of her shoulder bag and opened a small blade. "These old locks are pretty easy." She stuck the blade in and jiggled it. "Come on," she urged. "Come on."

Mo heard the click.

"Piece of cake," Lashandra said, grinning.

"Don't you need a search warrant or something?"

Lashandra glanced at Mo, eyebrow raised. She turned the handle and pushed the door. It didn't yield. "Warped," she muttered. Lashandra wrenched the handle, at the same time slamming her hip into the door. It opened with a shriek.

"Glad we're not trying to sneak up on anybody," she said, stepping back so Mo could enter first.

The sunset had left a lingering glow, but inside, the hall was dark. Lashandra again fished in her bag, lifting out a long-handled flashlight.

"You got a kitchen sink in there, too?"

"I might. I'm afraid to dig too deep."

Lashandra combed the beam of light back and forth at their feet as she and Mo crept slowly into the hall.

"Do you think we'll find any footprints?" Mo whispered.

"None or too many. Why are we whispering?"

"I don't know. There's nobody here but the ghosts of old council members."

They edged up the right side of the hall. The floor was littered with sawdust and small pieces of unpainted wood. The smell of fresh lumber mingled with the musk. Mo almost tripped over an extension cord, which slithered toward the front of the hall under Lashandra's light.

When they reached the side door, Lashandra squatted down.

"Anything?"

"This could be part of a boot print. Hold the light. Right here. See that?"

"Not really."

"It's about the right size."

Mo sensed something shifting in the stale air around her. She struggled to keep the light steady while Lashandra compared the partial boot print with the pictures she had taken at the school.

"No go," she said, standing up.

" 'No go' you can't tell, or 'no go' they don't match?"

"They don't match. The person who left this print isn't the same person who stood behind the tree."

"It was a long shot."

"Yep. Let's go eat."

Mo drove them back through town and out the highway to Adamski's. Only three cars dotted the parking lot, and Mo recognized one as the Adamskis'. The big dining room was almost empty. A middle-aged man and woman Mo didn't know occupied one of the tables in the center of the room, and a group of six overfilled a booth across the room on the highway side.

They took a booth along the back wall, where they could look out at the darkness where the river bowed to form Lake Maunesha. The large menus were pinned between the wall and the wire holder housing ketchup, mustard, salt, pepper, and packets of sugar.

"Corn fritters." Lashandra said, studying the menu. "I haven't had those since I moved up north."

"They serve them with fruit compote. They're really good."

"What are you kids up to tonight?"

Mo looked up into Horace Adamski's smiling face. "Hey, Horace," she said, smiling back. "Where's Martha?"

"She's in the back, cooking. You're stuck with me." He placed large glasses of ice water by their place settings.

"You two have met, right?" Mo nodded toward Lashandra.

"How are you, Mr. Adamski?" Lashandra leaned out to shake his hand.

"Overworked, underpaid, and undernourished. Nobody loves me, and my feet hurt. Think I'll go out in the garden and eat worms. How are you keeping, detective?"

"Very well, thank you. Hungry."

"You've come to the right place. You gonna try Martha's fritters?"

"I've narrowed it down to the fritters or the meatloaf."

"Have the fritters. You can come back for a cold meatloaf sandwich tomorrow. It's better the second day."

"Fritters it is." She closed the menu.

"I'll have the meatloaf," Mo said. "Tomorrow may never come."

"You'd better eat dessert first, then, in case the world ends."

"That's okay. After Martha's meatloaf, I won't be able to eat a LifeSaver. And…"

"I know. Hold the gravy." He shook his head. "It's a sacrilege."

"Nice place," Lashandra said after he retreated to the kitchen to give Martha their order.

"It's what passes for fine dining in Mitchell."

"Say, listen. I'm sorry we got off on the wrong foot. I might have been a tad judgmental."

"You mean we small-town hicks aren't so bad after all?"

"I deserve that."

"Not really. I'm sorry, too."

"Okay. Good."

"There's something I wanted to ask you. About the case."

"Fire away."

"It's something Joey Hasslebaum told me." Mo took a long sip of her ice water. "Did the murderer really carve a cross on Father O's chest?"

"Somebody carved something. It could have been a cross, and we assume the murderer did it. It was done after Father O'Bannon was already dead."

"What do you think it means?"

"When a killer does something like that, he—or she—is usually making a statement. Your guess is as good as mine, probably better, as to what that statement might be. I suppose it could be some sort of protest against the Catholic Church."

Horace brought their food, and they ate in silence for a time. Mo heard a noise behind her and turned. She choked on a bite of mashed potato, and Lashandra leaned over, hand raised to thump her on the back.

"I'm okay," Mo rasped. She took a sip of water. "Look behind me," she said, glancing over her shoulder.

Leona Dudley bent over the table across the room, piling dirty plates and glasses into a plastic tub. She began swabbing the table with a damp cloth, her back to them.

"Isn't that the woman from the church?" Lashandra asked. "What's she doing here?"

Finished with her cleaning, Leona Dudley hoisted the plastic tub and walked toward the kitchen, her eyes averted.

"Well, hi, you two," Martha Adamski said as she burst through the swinging kitchen door and headed toward them, brushing past Leona Dudley. "Horace told me you were out here. So nice to see you. How is everything tonight? Looks like you're cleaning your plates. How's Douglas? Things working out okay with that new job?"

"He's fine. He loves the new job."

"You tell him I said 'hi,' will you?"

"I sure will. Thanks. Does Leona Dudley work here now?"

"Yep. We put her on after the church had to let her go. And good thing we did. She's the only one can get that old Hammond dishwasher to run."

"I didn't know she'd been laid off."

"With nobody living at the rectory, they really didn't need a housekeeper. We give her as many hours as we can, but…" Martha looked around the nearly empty room. "Except for Friday and Saturday nights, we don't need a lot of help this time of year, as you can see. It'll be pretty tame until we start getting the deer hunters and snowmobilers. You folks save room for a nice piece of pie?"

Lashandra held her hand up. "No, ma'am."

"We're good, Martha. Thanks."

"I'll figure out the damages, then." She fished around in her apron pocket and took out her pad. "We're letting poor Leona stay with us at the house while her husband's up north. She's never liked to stay home alone, poor soul, and now that there's nobody at the rectory, she doesn't want to stay there, either. Let's see. That's the fritters and the meatloaf platter." Martha jabbed at the pad with a stubby pencil.

"Where's Mr. Dudley?" Mo asked.

"He works the cranberry harvest this time every year. He comes back for a day or so sometimes, to keep tabs on Leona. Should be finished up there any time now. He'll be here a couple of weeks, and then off he'll go deer hunting up north with his drinkin' buddies. I don't know how she puts up with him.

"Here you go, then. I'll take 'er up at the register for you when you're ready."

Martha slapped the ticket face down on the table and hurried off.

"This one's mine," Lashandra said, covering the check with her hand. "You got that glorious mess of breakfast at the diner the other day."

"I won't make a scene," Mo said.

"What's the matter? You looked flummoxed, as my daddy used to say."

"If Albert Dudley has been up north working the cranberry harvest, and Leona doesn't stay at home alone, she must have been staying at the rectory the night Father O was murdered."

Lashandra balled up her napkin and dropped it on her plate. "She lied to us."

"And she went through that whole business about calling her husband to get a ride, when she knew very well he wasn't there."

"That is curious." Lashandra shook her head. "I certainly haven't been thinking of her as a suspect."

"She couldn't have killed Father O." Mo looked around.

Three couples occupied tables now, but no one seemed to have heard her. "But why would she lie?" she said in a quieter voice.

"A woman staying alone in a house with a man? A priest at that? I don't know about this town, but where I come from, tongues would be wagging. That could explain it."

"Leona Dudley and Father O. Come on, Lashandra. Besides, if Martha knew about the arrangement, it couldn't have been a secret."

"I guess there's only one way to sort it all out." Lashandra slid across the bench and stood up. "Let's go talk to Mrs. Dudley."

Mo's heart sank. Poor Leona. The first interview had seemed to be almost too much for her. How would she react to more questions now?

Lashandra was already walking across the dining room. Before she could reach the kitchen, the door swung open, and Horace emerged, carrying a large tray with two steaming platters of food on it.

"Would it be all right if I had a few words with Mrs. Dudley?" Lashandra asked him.

"It's fine by me, but she ain't here. She said she was feeling poorly and asked if she could go home early. I said 'sure.' There's nothing here we can't handle. I can ring her up for you when she gets to the house if you want."

"It can wait. Thanks."

"How'd you like them fritters?"

"Fantastic."

"Told you. Get here early for lunch tomorrow. The meatloaf'll be gone by twelve thirty."

Mo waited until they were back in the car before talking again. "Something still bothers me about that cross," she said as she maneuvered out of the parking lot and back onto the county highway.

"What's that?"

"What you said, about the murder maybe being some sort of protest against the Catholic Church. Couldn't it be the other way around?"

"Meaning...?"

"Couldn't the murderer think he was somehow avenging the Church for something Father O had done? Some supposed offense against the Church?"

"I suppose it could work either way."

"If it's the same person, what was he avenging by trying to burn the ballpark down? Steve Everson isn't even Catholic."

"It's much more likely that it's two different people. We really have no evidence linking the two."

Mo slowed as they reached Main Street and pulled in next to Lashandra's car. "You'll have to talk to Leona Dudley again, won't you?"

"Actually, I was thinking maybe you should talk to her."

"Really?"

"She knows you, trusts you." Their eyes met briefly. "You game?"

"Yeah. Sure."

"I thought you would be."

Mo stood and watched until Lashandra's car had rounded the curve where Main Street turned back into the county highway. She had jumped at the chance to talk to Leona, but she dreaded having to make her delve into such a painful subject again.

The thought seemed monstrous, but what if Leona were somehow implicated in Father O's murder? Would Mo be put in the position of having to bring this sweet old woman to justice?

She shook off the thought. There was nothing to do now but to play it to the end and accept the truth, whatever it turned out to be.

Doug had breakfast ready–mushroom omelets and a fruit salad–when she got up the next morning. They ate in front of a fire in the living room, the first of the season. Doug had something funky playing softly on the stereo.

"You really should taste it before you salt it," he said.

The salt shaker hovered above her plate. Jackie watched from the floor.

"I just like it a little spicier than you do."

"I spiced it up this time, honest."

Mo put the shaker on the low table between them and ate a bite of omelet. It needed salt.

"How is it?"

"It's fine."

"Want some coffee?"

"Please. What's that we're listening to?"

"Cephas and Wiggins. *Somebody Told the Truth*. Like it?"

"I'm not sure yet. It's a little early in the morning." She looked at the omelet, dug her fork in for a bite, dropped the fork on the floor, and cried.

"What's the matter?"

Doug was out of his chair and hovering over her. She

wanted to assure him that she was all right, but sobs shook her. His arm curled around her shoulders as he knelt by her chair. He stroked her hair, and she gave in to the crying. Then it was as if she were watching herself cry, and the tears stopped.

"I have no idea what that was all about," she said, wishing he'd unwrap her so she could sit up.

"It's not a big mystery. Somebody murdered your priest. You've been too busy to mourn him. The whole thing just caught up with you. That's all."

"I'm glad I'm so easy to figure out."

"I don't mean it that way. I'm just saying I think you're entitled to your tears."

"Your food's getting cold."

"So's yours."

His arm withdrew from her, and he stood.

"Jack Roosevelt Robinson!"

Doug had put his plate on the floor when he'd gotten up, and Jackie was licking the omelet. He hissed when Doug scooped him up. "At least the cat likes my cooking," he said as he marched off to the kitchen. "You've got a perfectly good breakfast of your own out here," he told the cat.

A knife clinked on a plate. The garbage disposal gargled. Doug returned and sat back in the armchair next to her.

"I wasn't crying about the omelet."

"I know."

The fire needed more wood, but Mo didn't want to ask him to tend to it, and she didn't feel like getting up.

"You're looking at me like you think I'll explode," she said.

"No, I'm not." He looked away.

She forced herself to take a bite of omelet.

"Oh, go ahead and salt it."

"Why don't you eat it? Please. I'm really not hungry."

He shrugged, took the plate and her fork, and ate a big bite of omelet. "Your fight's with God," he said, his mouth not quite empty, "not with me."

"Which shouldn't be a problem, since God doesn't exist, right?"

"Makes him tough to beat. You keep right on praying, and God keeps right on not answering. I'd think you'd get tired of it after a while."

"He answers, Doug. Sometimes it isn't the answer we want."

"Then what's the good of praying? Besides, I thought the Bible says that if you ask, you'll receive."

"'Seek, and you shall find. Knock, and the door shall be opened unto you.' Jesus says that right after He teaches the disciples the Lord's Prayer."

"So, you get whatever you ask for, as long as you ask for what God already wants to give you."

"God gives us what we need."

"Then why ask?" Doug scooped up a forkful of omelet and shoved it into his mouth.

"Maybe we shouldn't have this discussion right now."

"We don't ever have to have it, as far as I'm concerned. You're the one who keeps bringing the subject up."

She bit back the angry words that flared up in her.

"I'm sorry, honey," Doug said. "I'm just sick of trying to get inside that cosmic tautology of yours. 'Everything happens because God wills it; ergo, everything that happens is proof of God's existence. God exists because He exists." He shrugged. "If you can believe that, that's great for you. I don't have your faith. I need proof."

"Faith isn't something you have, Doug. It's something you do. You live faith."

"Act as if you believe long enough, and you start believing? That sounds like brainwashing to me."

She picked up her coffee mug and brought it to her lips, but suddenly the idea of trying to ingest anything else sickened her. "You know what?" she said, putting the mug down on the table harder than she'd intended. "Right now, I don't really care what it sounds like to you. Are you finished with that?" She nodded toward the plate in his lap. "I'll get the dishes."

"That's okay. I'll do them."

"I'll do the dishes, Doug. You're already feeling martyred because I didn't eat your breakfast."

Her hands in hot, soapy water, Mo regretted her harsh words and the bewildered, hurt look they produced on Doug. When they argued, he became a shy, needy little boy.

He'd managed to burn the omelet pan. Mo let it soak while she straightened up the kitchen, then attacked the pan with abrasive and scouring pad. The combination of hot water and hard scrubbing soothed her, and having the kitchen tidy satisfied her.

Blest are the peacemakers, she thought. How very short of the mark I fall in that regard.

Mo found Doug in his office, shoulders hunched before the computer screen. She stood in the doorway for a few moments, not sure if he were absorbed in what he was doing or ignoring her.

"Doug?"

He turned from the screen, frowning. "I'm sorry. What I said was uncalled for."

"Oh, I probably called for it. I'm just uptight because you'll be gone this weekend."

"And maybe just a wee bit upset because I'll be seeing

Cynthia, if only for a few minutes when I pick up Lawrence."

"I'm excited for you, Doug. I really am. You get to take your son to a World Series game at Wrigley Field."

"It's a dream come true." He took a deep breath. "I respect your faith. I'm probably just envious."

She crossed the room, stood behind him, and massaged his shoulders. The muscles were knotted hard beneath her fingers.

"Work?" she asked.

"No. I'm checking out a chat room Steve told me about. 'War and Peace.' He's trying to make a pacifist out of me, which is probably why I went off on you about religion."

Mo leaned in, continuing to massage his shoulder muscles, and watched the screen fill with lines of dialogue. She avoided chat rooms, thinking them a waste of time at best, vaguely dangerous at worst. It troubled her a bit to find Doug involved in one now, even one on such an important topic.

"That feels good. Thanks," he said.

The speeches on the screen were attributed to 'Dixiechik,' 'Madbomber,' 'Shockn'odd,' 'Hippie burnout,' and other colorful aliases. A name at the top of the screen caught her eye just as it disappeared.

"Wait. Could you scroll back up?"

"Sure."

The dialogue backed up.

" 'Weasel'?"

"Yeah. He's a regular. Thinks we should bomb hell out of anybody who doesn't agree with us, including France. You get some real kooks on here. I can't see why Steve bothers with it. Actually, he mentioned Weasel when he told me about the chat room. Apparently they really got into it a few weeks back."

"Steve and Weasel?"

"Yeah. Big time. He said Weasel threatened to do him bodily harm. Which is a good reason to use a screen name, huh?"

"What's Steve's?"

"'Maverick.' He said he'd be on this morning, but I don't see him. There are about twenty five on now. Steve says they get a hundred sometimes, and it gets really nuts."

"Can you find out who any of these people really are?"

Doug scratched his thatch of black hair. He'd just gotten a haircut, and he reminded her of a fuzzy chick. "Sure. We're using instant messaging. The screen name is also the email address."

"What about a name?"

"There are online directories, but it's like the phone book. You need the name to get the email address. It helps if you have at least the state, too. Otherwise, if it's a common name, you get hundreds of matches."

He closed the chat room screen and clicked on a web site called "Switchboard." Boxes formed on the screen, asking him to fill in last name, first name, city and state. He typed in "Quinn," then "Monona," and then "Mitchell," and scanned down the state list, clicking on "Wisconsin."

In seconds her full name, address, and phone number appeared on the screen. Underneath, a blue line asked if he wanted to search for an email address. To the side, a box listed "Credit rating," "Social Security information," "Police records…"

"Whoa. This thing does background checks?"

"Sure. There's another site where you can access FBI files under the Freedom of Information Act. I run checks for clients who are thinking of investing in small businesses."

Mo watched while Doug typed in his own name and got

the results, again in seconds. "Want to check to see if I've got any warrants out on me?"

"What if you wanted to go backward, from email to address?"

"I'm not sure how you'd do that."

"There's a directory that lets you go from address or phone number to name. Reporters use it all the time."

"And detectives, I bet." He shot her a look over his shoulder. "Which are you being?"

"Neither. I'm just curious. Type in 'Juan Ortega' and 'Mitchell.'"

"You want to find out if Ortega has a police record?"

"Nope. Just his phone number."

"There you go."

Mo repeated the number to herself twice. "I'm going to call him from the other line."

She repeated the number as she walked through the living room and punched the number in on the kitchen phone.

"Hello?"

"Señor Ortega? This is Mo Quinn. I hope I'm not disturbing you."

"Not at all. It is a pleasure to hear your voice. What can I do for you?"

"I was wondering about that young man you mentioned who came to the Tridentine Mass a few weeks ago."

"The little fellow with the backpack and the notebook?"

"Yes. I was wondering if you had happened to check the guest book for his name."

"I did. I meant to call you. I think it started with a D. Just a second… Olivia," Mo heard him call, his hand over the mouthpiece. "What was the name of that little fellow with the backpack and the boots?

"Just a second," he said. "She's coming."

"Did you say boots?"

"Yes. He had those ankle-high boots that lace all the way up, like they wear in the Army. I remember thinking he must be baking his feet, to wear such things in the summer. Just a second."

Mo heard a muffled conversation on the other end of the line.

"She says his name was Baser or Beser. His handwriting is hard to read. The first name starts with a B, too. Bayard, it looks like."

"That's great, Señor Ortega. Thanks so much."

"It is something important, Señora Quinn?"

"I don't know. It might be. I sure appreciate your help."

"I'm happy to be of service."

Doug was back in the 'War and Peace' chat room when she returned to his office.

"Could we go back to Switchboard? I have a name I'd like to try."

"Be my guest."

He got up and stretched while Mo slid into the chair. She accessed Switchboard, typed in Baser and "Mitchell" and failed to get a match. She also failed to get a match using "Madison" for the city. The same happened with Beser.

"Now what?" Doug asked from over her shoulder.

"Maybe it's 'z'."

"Maybe what's 'z'?"

"Bezer. Spanish speakers pronounce 'z' like 's.' I might have written it down wrong."

Mo typed in Bezer and Mitchell and again failed to get a match. She substituted Madison for Mitchell and tried again. After a short wait, the screen produced "Bayard Bezer IV" with a Madison street address and phone number.

Mo fumbled with the mouse and clicked on the email search. Her heart pounded as she waited. "Weasel@aol. com" appeared on the screen.

"There you are," Doug said. "You found our little warmonger. Can you believe that name? No wonder he calls himself 'Weasel.'"

Mo clicked on "print," and Doug's printer whirred into motion.

"Mind telling me what this is all about?"

"Nothing, probably. The name 'Weasel' came up in another context."

"As in a murder investigation context? Should you be turning whatever you're finding over to that detective before you get assaulted again?"

"It's probably nothing."

"You don't sound like it's nothing." He turned her around in the chair and put a hand on each shoulder. "You think this guy might be the killer, don't you?"

Mo nodded. "I do."

"Call the detective. Right now."

"Okay. I will."

"Why do you think this Weasel makes a good murder suspect?"

Lashandra had to raise her voice over the diner din. With a University of Wisconsin football game scheduled at Camp Randall across the street in less than three hours, Mickey's Dairy Bar was even more crowded than usual for a Saturday morning. Throngs of red-clad fans streamed past the window, seeming to march to the driving drum cadence of the Badger marching band warming up nearby.

"Father O told me."

Lashandra arched an eyebrow.

"A passage he had marked in his Bible started me thinking about persecuted peacemakers. Father O and Steve Everson both protested the war, and we can connect Weasel to both of them."

Lashandra glanced around and leaned over the table. "Here's our problem. No judge is going to issue a search warrant on the basis of a Bible quotation, and we don't have enough to pull Weasel in for questioning."

"Can't you do a stakeout or something?"

Lashandra laughed. "We don't actually do a lot of that.

If we tried to watch everybody we thought might be up to something, we wouldn't be able to do anything else."

"But this guy might be a killer."

"You want coffee?"

"Yes, please." Mo flipped her mug up, and the waitress —not the same one who had served her when she was with Naomi—expertly directed a stream of coffee into it from a foot above the rim.

"Do you have ice tea?" Lashandra asked.

"I think we can manage that. You ready to order?"

"Pancakes," Mo said. "Short stack."

"Could I have two eggs, over easy, and wheat toast, dry?"

"You bet. You want yanks with that?"

"Yanks?"

"Yes, she wants yanks."

"Oh, yeah. Yanks. I want yanks."

"You guys here for the game?"

"I don't even know who they're playing," Mo said.

"Upper Iowa State Teachers College for Nuns. They don't like to schedule anything too challenging for the last pre-conference game."

The waitress moved off, coffeepot at the ready.

"I can't believe this place," Lashandra said. "I might have lived in Madison for decades and never discovered it."

"Mickey's is definitely wonderful."

"So I see." She folded her hands together on the table. "I've got to admit, Weasel looks like a good fit for the Mansfield Park arson, since he obviously had something going with Everson. But murdering a priest because he's for peace?"

"People kill abortion doctors in the name of sanctity of life."

The waitress plunked Lashandra's iced tea in front of her and whisked off. In the next booth, a group of college-aged men exploded into laughter, and a ripe obscenity cut through the noise.

"Nice talk," Lashandra muttered. "You hear stuff on the streets now that would made Satan blush." She took a long sip of her iced tea. "And that's from the coeds."

"We know Weasel attended the Latin Mass," Mo said while Lashandra dumped two packets of sugar into her tea. "He could have found Frankie's knife and used it to kill Father O."

"Why would he kill Father O but not Everson?"

"Maybe he just hasn't had the chance yet."

The waitress came back with their food and gave Mo a refill on her coffee.

"My Lord," Lashandra said. "Are those pancakes?"

"I know. And they're so good."

Lashandra poked her steaming potatoes with a fork. "Funky, chunky hash browns." She peppered her eggs liberally, stirred in some of the yanks, and forked in a big bite. "Delicious... If Weasel really is our guy, and I'm not saying I'm convinced, I sure don't want to wait until he kills Everson before we do something."

Mo took a bite of pancake and dabbed at her mouth with her napkin. "What if we could match the boot print you found at St. Anne's with the boots Weasel wears?"

Lashandra thought about that. "It would probably be enough to get a warrant." She looked up into Mo's intense face. "You want to go find where this guy lives and look for boot prints right now, don't you?"

"Well, yeah."

"Can I finish my breakfast first?"

"Of course."

†††

They had to park two blocks away from the address Mo had found on the Internet. They walked along the tree-shaded sidewalk. Paper and plastic cups littered the lawns, and a beer keg tilted drunkenly on one of the porches.

"Looks like it was party time last night," Mo said.

"The party starts Wednesday afternoon around here. I wouldn't want to be a foot cop working State Street tonight."

Like its neighbors, the ratty two-story wood-frame house that matched the address in Mo's search had suffered years of neglect. It had been subdivided into apartments and rented out to students. A sign in one of the downstairs windows advised passersby that "Regime change begins at home."

Lashandra strode across the lawn and took the porch steps two at a time, with Mo right behind her. The porch held a filthy, torn couch. A plastic cup, half full of stale beer, perched on the porch railing. Two rolled-up newspapers leaned against the door.

"No buzzers," Lashandra noted. "And the mailboxes don't have names on 'em."

"What now?"

"Let's look over there." The detective nodded toward a tangle of bicycles at the side of the house, attached by chains to a rusting bike rack that listed about 15 degrees.

The weedy stubble of lawn had been worn to smooth dirt around the rack. Lashandra squatted. She inched around the perimeter, studying at the scuffed dirt.

"Anything?"

"Take a look. That could be part of the same heel."

"Yes. I see it."

"There's nothing here that does us any good, though. Come on."

They moved around to the back of the house, where a weed-infested yard held two drooping apple trees. Bird-pecked apples littered the ground.

Lashandra nodded toward an upstairs window, where a "Support Our Troops" sign hung behind a filthy pane of glass. "I'll bet that's our guy's room."

"You don't see too many of those signs in downtown Madison," Mo said.

"Unless you want to toss pebbles at this window to see if he's in, I think that's about all we can do."

"No search warrant?"

"No search warrant."

†††

Lashandra dropped Mo off at her car near the diner.

"Sorry we didn't do better," Lashandra said. "I'll be in touch."

Sitting in her car, Mo watched Lashandra drive off. She put the key in the ignition, took it out again. A wave of fatigue and loneliness washed over her, leaving her light-headed. She would have gone to her self–defense class, but Suzanne cancelled on football Saturdays. Mo had no place to go but an empty house or an empty office.

She got out of the car and walked toward campus. Crowds drank beer in an area marked off with low metal barriers across from Camp Randall, and the smell of grilling bratwurst permeated the crisp fall air.

She thought about Doug with his son in Chicago, looking forward to their first World Series game—and the first appearance for the Cubs in a World Series in almost six decades. Steve had given him the tickets, bless him, and Mo had insisted that Doug take Lawrence. She prayed that they would have a good time but stopped short of asking God for a Cub victory.

Instead, as she walked, she prayed she might be a more understanding, less jealous wife. She would always have to share Doug with his ex-wife. He and Cynthia had made two children together, and no matter what had happened to their relationship, Doug loved his kids and worked hard to be a part of their lives.

A sad thing, she thought, when parents went to war. She wondered how she might be one of those blessed peace-makers Jesus spoke of.

She walked all the way to the Memorial Union and out onto the terrace overlooking Lake Mendota. A few sailboats dotted the far side of the lake, and several boats bobbed at their moorings close to shore. Soon a thick sheet of ice would coat that lake. She shivered, wishing she'd brought her jacket with her from the car.

Then she was walking again, up Langdon Street, past the stately old armory and the fraternity and soror-ity houses, where students sat on porches drinking beer or passed footballs back and forth on the lawn, while the report of the game murmured from radios.

Her own college days seemed to belong to another era. Mo remembered both heart-wrenching loneliness and the joy of belonging. The young lady she had been would surely be surprised to find herself married to a financial consul-tant and editing a community newspaper in a little farm town.

She walked faster against a chill that sank into her bones. Reaching the end of Langdon Street, with the Edge-water Hotel and the lake on her left, she turned right onto Wisconsin Avenue and walked toward the Capitol several blocks ahead.

She hadn't been to the library or the Historical Society Museum in a long time. She'd never been to the Veterans Museum. She could browse the bookstores on State Street. She could even go to a matinee. She hadn't done that in years. Why not spend the day in Madison? Until what? What was she waiting for?

The Middle of Midnight. The thought made her stop. The title of one of the books Father O had left her. He had been killed in the middle of the night, sometime around midnight. The fire at Mansfield Park had started in the middle of the night. If the same person had been responsible for both, perhaps he made a habit of roaming at midnight.

And if he did, that would mean that his apartment would be empty.

Did she really dare to break into Weasel's apartment?

Of course not, she told herself. That would be as stupid as it was illegal. She'd just take a look around. Maybe there'd be someone around she could talk to, someone who knew this Weasel and could tell her something that would allay—or confirm—her suspicions.

She'd be careful. She'd promised Doug. And besides, she had no stomach for confronting another killer.

At the corner of Park and University, throngs of drinkers spilled out into the sidewalk from the bar. The World Series played on the screen inside. Mo eased her way through the crowd, drawing appreciative stares from many of the young males. Derek Lowe was pitching, with Alex Gonzales at bat.

"What's the score?" she asked a young man who seemed to be watching the game.

"Where you been?" he said. "The Badgers won."

"No. I mean the baseball game."

"What baseball game?"

She asked two more patrons, drawing a "Who cares?" and a shrug.

"Looks like you need a drink, pretty lady."

The grinning young man looked to be all of 19 or 20. He clutched an empty beer mug in one hand, a lit cigarette in the other.

"You're about to burn your fingers."

"Whassat?"

"Your cigarette. It's about to burn your fingers."

"Oh. Yeah. Thanks." He dropped the cigarette and

mashed it with his foot. "So?" His smile was relentless, his eyes not quite focused. "Whattaya drinking?"

"I'm drinking in the incredible optimism of youth."

"Howsat?"

She worked her way through the crowd and back to the street, where she gulped down fresh air. She pulled up the hood of her parka, again wishing for her jacket, and began walking east on University, away from the center of campus.

It was time.

She'd had no problem passing the day in downtown Madison, ending her afternoon with a nice dinner at The White Horse near the Arts Center and thoroughly enjoying a first-run movie with Robert Duvall in the gorgeous, old Orpheum Theater.

But now she was exhausted. She would have loved to be home, snug in her bed, with Jackie curled up in the crook of her knees.

She was also scared. She had to admit it. What had seemed plausible, even slightly reasonable, in the daylight, now seemed insane.

She could turn around, walk back to her car and go home, she reminded herself. She kept walking. She knew where she was going. She just didn't know what she'd do when she got there.

Music flowed out of the houses. Porches sagged under laughing young men and women. She didn't remember any of the street names, and everything looked different in the dark. Yet she never hesitated, walking straight to the house, with its tilting bike rack, its weedy backyard, its two sagging apple trees.

A light burned dimly in the window behind the "Support the Troops" sign. Weasel was home. Now what?

As if in answer, the light blinked out.

She hurried back around the house and crouched in the shadows by the porch. She heard heavy footsteps, and a short man passed through the open doorway, his boots thudding on the porch. He wore a tattered army jacket and clutched a torn canvas backpack. The overhead light glistened off his skull, which was covered with a brown stubble of hair. She couldn't see his face but saw that he wore glasses. He thundered down the steps and walked diagonally across the lawn.

Mo took a tentative step after him, then stopped, watching as he walked out of sight down the sidewalk.

Mounting the porch steps, she made herself take a deep breath, then another. She slipped inside the open door into a dimly lit hallway.

A door to her left flew open, and a lean, young black man, wearing only tattered jeans, emerged.

"Excuse me." he said, stepping back.

"You startled me."

"Sorry. I thought you were my roommate." His grin seemed boyish, innocent. "You're definitely not my roommate."

Mo's mind seemed to have gone silent. She could think of nothing to say, no pretext for being there.

The man folded his arms across his bare chest. "I'm not dressed for company."

He was a nice looking young man, with a sweet smile and unblemished skin. He was some mother's dear baby boy, gone off to college and all alone on a Saturday night.

"My name's Mo," the young man said. "Short for Maurice."

"You're kidding."

"Would I kid about being named Maurice?"

"My name's Mo. Monona."

"My gosh. It's fate. We were destined to meet."

"Is that why you didn't go out partying with your room-mate?"

He shrugged. "I wanted to watch the World Serious. Lifelong Red Sox fan. There's no known cure."

She laughed at the 'serious.' "I've got the Cubs strain of the virus. My husband's infected, too. He's at the game."

"Then he's a mighty happy man. The Cubs won."

"You're kidding."

"Wouldn't kid about that, either." He frowned. "But you can't have a husband. We're destined to be together. Mo and Mo."

"A Cubs fan and a Red Sox fan? It would never work out."

A woman's shrill laughter reached them from down the street.

"Do you know the man who lives upstairs?" It was out before she knew she was going to ask.

"Can't say that I know him. I hear him tromp up and down the stairs. He went out just before you came. He goes out about this time every night." He frowned again. "I know. You're from homeland security. This guy is some kind of psycho terrorist."

Mo laughed, but her heart was pounding, and she felt lightheaded again.

"Why don't you just break into his apartment? It's right up there. First door at the top of the stairs."

"No, actually, I can come back..."

He shrugged, scratching at his hair. "Suit yourself." He stuck out his hand. "Very pleased to meet you, Mo. Sorry our karma thing didn't work out."

"Nice to meet you, too, Mo."

"May the better team win, huh?"

"How's that?"

"The World Serious? May the better team win."

"Right. Yes."

"Or maybe neither team will win. Maybe the world will end during the ninth inning of the seventh game. Fire shall rain from the sky. The earth shall tremble. The sheep shall be separated from the goats." He winked. "Hope we both turn out to be sheep." He slipped back into his room. The door clicked shut.

Mo looked up the stairs. The upper hallway was dimly lit. She heard music and laughter from down the street behind her.

She started up the stairs.

What are you doing? She thought it over and over, the words keeping time with her soft footfalls. She stopped at the top of the stairway. The door was across a narrow, dingy hall. She heard a voice. From a radio inside the room, she decided. She heard another sound, a cat meowing behind the door. She took a step, another, reached out, tried the doorknob.

The knob's resistance sent a shock up her arm.

That's that, she told herself. It's locked. Time to go home.

She turned to leave. He was standing at the foot of the stairs, the strap of his backpack slung over his shoulder, his eyes wide behind the thick lenses of his glasses.

"I heard what you said to the African," he said.

He was short and slight. His skin had the unhealthy pallor of someone who rarely saw the sun. He wore an army jacket with the word "Sachs" on a patch over the left breast. The jacket hung loosely on him. He wore a greasy baseball cap, its logo illegible from wear and grime.

"I was just leaving," Mo said.

"Don't be silly. You came to see me, didn't you?"

"Yes, I… No… I really do have to be going."

The little man swung his backpack off his shoulder and

dropped it at his feet. He stood blocking the steps, hands on hips. The voice droned on from the radio behind her.

"Why do you call yourself 'Weasel'?" she heard herself ask.

"Don't you like the name?"

"It's unusual."

"Beats 'Fuck Face,' don't you think?" He grabbed the strap of his backpack and began dragging it behind him up the stairs. "I've been called 'Weasel' or 'Fuck Face' as long as I can remember."

"Kids can be very cruel."

"I'm talking about my father."

He took another step, and another. The dim light in the stairwell glinted off his polished black boots. His eyes swam behind their thick lenses.

"What else would you like to know about me? We'll have a nice talk. That's what you came for, isn't it? To talk to me?"

"I really can't stay."

"Of course you'll stay. We'll have our talk."

He reached the top of the stairs. Blocking the stairs with his body, he fished a key out of his jacket pocket, then stepped forward and rattled the key in the lock.

"Come in. Come in. Welcome to my humble home."

He stood back, nodding toward the open door. She stepped in.

"I call this the war room. I'm afraid it's a little messy."

A narrow path of bare floor snaked through mounds of boxes, books, magazines, newspapers, drifts of paper, loose- leaf binders, notebooks. Against the far wall, a low table overflowed with more paper, piled around a computer and keyboard, a radio, and other electronic gear.

"You're listening to *Dreamscape*," the voice on the radio

said, "and we're live, coast to coast. I'm on the line now with Gerald in Denver."

She heard the door shut behind her, wood rasping on wood.

"Damn humidity. Makes the door swell up. I can barely get it shut."

"This is quite a set up."

"Thank you. It's my communications center. Everything is state of the art."

Something skittered in the papers at her feet, and she jumped back, almost falling.

"That's just Pumpkin. She's not very sociable. In fact, I'm the only one she'll have anything to do with."

Something orange and furry disappeared behind a bookshelf.

"Sit down. Please." He swept books and papers off an overstuffed couch. "I'm afraid I don't have much to offer you. I think there's some Dr. Pepper in the fridge."

"No. No, thank you."

"I've got grapefruit juice. How about a nice glass of grapefruit juice?"

"I'm fine. Really."

"Sit down. Sit down. Be comfortable. I know." He rummaged around in one of the pockets of his oversized army jacket. "Have a LifeSaver. Do you like LifeSavers?"

She tested the couch with her hand and sat carefully. He tossed his backpack on the floor, swung the chair around and sat down. He peeled the outer label from the tube of LifeSavers, folded it neatly in fourths, and put it in his pocket. Then he peeled the foil from the top of the tube of candy and extended it toward her. Mo leaned forward and accepted a LifeSaver.

"My name's Bayard," he said. "How's that for a handle, huh? My mother calls me Bebe." His voice was deep and much too big for his body. "And your name's Monona. Friends call you Mo."

"How do you know that?"

"I heard you tell the African. What does your mother call you, Monona?" He held up a hand, palm out. "That was rude, wasn't it? Sorry. I say socially inappropriate things sometimes. That's what my counselor says. She says I have a borderline personality disorder. ADD. Asperger's Syndrome." He laughed. "Don't you think that's a funny word, Monona? 'Asperger'?" He shook his head, waving the question away. "My counselor doesn't think it's funny, either."

He leaned forward. "Go ahead. Eat your LifeSaver. It isn't poisoned."

She put the circle of sugar in her mouth.

"And you," he said, "were very popular in high school. You got good grades and went to a good college. Nobody ever told you you had Asperger's or any other syndrome."

He stood up quickly, the chair thudding into the desk. The computer screen flashed on, a pale blue desktop cluttered with icons. Monona tensed, ready to spring up. A screech of static escaped the police scanner on the table.

"All units," a woman's voice said. "We've got a couple of drunks brawling on the sidewalk in the five hundred block of State Street. Who's close?"

He reached back and snapped the unit off. "They sent you here to spy on me, didn't they?"

"What makes you say a thing like that?" She risked a quick glance to her left, hoping to spot something she could use as a weapon. Her mouth was so dry, the LifeSaver hadn't started to melt yet.

"It's true, isn't it?"

"No. Nobody sent me, Bayard."

"Don't call me that."

"What do you want me to call you?"

"I don't want you to call me anything, Monona. I wanted you to leave me alone. But it's too late for that now, isn't it?"

"The police know about you. They'll be coming here soon."

"You're lying." He plopped back into his chair. He seemed almost wistful, and Mo was struck by how young he was.

"Why did you kill Father O'Bannon?"

"Who? Oh, yeah. Him."

"He was a wonderful man."

He jumped up again. Mo leapt to her feet, hands raised, legs spread, knees flexed.

He laughed. "That's too wonderful. You're going to beat me up!"

She stood unmoving, watching him, every muscle tensed. She swallowed the LifeSaver whole.

"You're a regular Charlie's Angel, Monona." He laughed again. He reached back, his hand waving in the air before contacting his chair. He fell back into the chair with a sigh. "What a country," he murmured. "What a country."

"Why did you kill him?"

He waited so long before answering, she almost asked again.

"Oh, Monona. Such a question. Sit down. Please. We were having such a nice chat. Do sit down, and I'll answer your question."

Mo sank slowly back into her chair, her eyes on him.

"Are you a Christian, Monona?"

She nodded.

"So you believe in doing what God tells you to do."

"Yes."

Bayard shrugged. "There you are. God told me to kill him. I did what He told me."

"How did God tell you that, Bayard? Did you hear a voice?"

He bent down and rummaged through his backpack, fishing out a spiral notebook. He put the notebook in his lap and began thumbing the pages covered with cramped printing in black ink.

"Are you afraid of me, Monona?" he asked without looking up. "Never mind. You'd just lie."

"I won't lie to you, Bayard."

"Why should you be any different than the rest of the human race?" He looked up at her. "Okay. Let's test your assertion. You promise you won't lie to me."

"That's right."

"Have you really told the police about me? Ah. See? You have to stop and think about it. That means you're making up a lie."

"I'm not. And yes, I told them about you. They know I'm here."

"That's a lie."

"You're right. That last part isn't true. I'm sorry."

"See how one lie just leads to another, Monona?"

"I've talked about you with a sheriff's detective. She was here with me earlier today. That's the truth."

"She? A lady cop?"

"A detective, yes."

He seemed to be studying her face. "Are you afraid of me, Monona? Don't lie."

"No. I'm not afraid of you."

"You should be. I could kill you."

"That's the thing about killing, Bayard. One just leads to another."

He smiled. "You're really not afraid."

"No."

"Why aren't you? Don't you think I'd kill you?"

"I'm not afraid to die."

"Really? How extraordinary." He leaned back, watching her. His eyes seemed to swim behind the thick lenses of his glasses. "You figure God will take you up to heaven, huh?"

"I don't know. I trust Him."

"You really are a Christian. I find that troubling."

"Why is that?"

"You seem intelligent."

"You don't think an intelligent person can be a Christian?"

"Must make it tough."

Mo glanced around the room, again looking for a weapon. Her muscles ached from tensing for so long.

"Do I disgust you, Monona?"

The question surprised her. "No," she said, shaking her head.

"Really? I don't scare you, and I don't disgust you. Isn't that remarkable?" He rubbed his forehead and took off his glasses to massage the bridge of his nose.

"Were you raised Catholic, Bayard?"

"I was indoctrinated, yes."

"But you've fallen away from the Church?"

"Fallen away. That's such a quaint phrase, isn't it? A fallen away Catholic. Lapsed. Like an overdue library book."

"I just meant…"

"I know what you meant. I'm not stupid."

"I don't think you're stupid. You seem quite intelligent to me." She had to fight to keep her voice calm. Every muscle in her body screamed for her to move.

"Do I? Quite intelligent. My, my. On what do you base that assessment?"

Something rustled to her right. Pumpkin had been creeping toward them. She froze, her eyes on Mo.

Bayard looked around the room. "This place is a mess," he said. He looked at her. "I'm sorry. You were saying?"

"Let me help you, Bayard."

He snorted, rearing back. "I don't want you to help me, Monona. I don't need your help. Why is it women always think they need to fix every man they meet?"

"I don't want to fix you, Bayard. You murdered a priest. You tried to burn down a ballpark. You're in big trouble. If you kill me, you'll be in bigger trouble."

"How many times can they kill me?"

"Is God telling you to kill me, Bayard?"

He frowned. "No, he isn't."

"What is He saying?"

"He isn't saying anything. He stopped talking hundreds of years ago." He stood up again, staring at something behind her, then sat down again. "So, you want to help me. Is that your deal?"

"That's my deal."

"Why would you want to do that?"

Something brushed her hand dangling over the side of the couch. Pumpkin rubbed her muzzle back and forth. Monona scratched behind the cat's ears, and Pumpkin purred.

"That's remarkable," Bayard said. "She never lets anyone touch her."

"Cats seem to like me."

"Speaks well for you. Do you have a cat?"

"Yes."

"What's your cat's name?"

"Jackie. Jack Roosevelt Robinson."

"After the baseball player."

"Yes."

He laughed. Pumpkin walked to the closed door, sat, and stared up at it as if expecting it to open.

"He's black, I take it. Your cat."

"Yes."

Pumpkin meowed. Bayard's smile faded. "Who'll take care of Pumpkin?" he asked.

"I will."

He looked at her. "Okay," he said at last. "Call that cop friend of yours. Detective. Lady detective."

"Her name is Lashandra. She's a good person."

"Lashandra. Is that a African name?"

"She's from Louisiana."

He seemed to consider that. "You can use my cell phone. It's state of the art."

"Thank you, Bayard."

"You're welcome, Monona."

He handed her the phone, and she punched in Lashandra's cell phone number from memory. While it rang, Pumpkin came back and rubbed up against her leg, asking to be petted.

21

The phone was ringing when Monona opened the front door. She charged into the kitchen and snatched up the receiver.

"Hello?"

"It's me. I'm at the rest stop just over the state line, so I'm about an hour from home."

"Was it fun?"

"Awesome. Sammy hit one out in dead center that hasn't come down yet."

She smiled. "Did Lawrence have a good time?"

"He really did. He tried not to get excited, but after a while, it was just like when he was a little kid."

"That's wonderful."

"Yeah. Anything happen on the home front?"

"Nothing on the magnitude of a Cubs win. I'll tell you when you get here."

"Good enough."

"Drive carefully."

"I will. Bye. I love you."

"I love you."

As soon as Mo hung up, she regretted not telling Doug

224 · Marshall Cook

about the arrest, but she dreaded having to admit that she had again been involved, had in fact again confronted a murderer, alone, in his apartment.

Something was nagging at her, had nagged at her the whole drive home from Madison. She felt no relief at having Father O's killer in custody, no sense of what the talk show hosts insisted on calling closure. When she thought of the poor, frightened little boy-man who had confessed to murder to her, she simply couldn't square the picture with the image of Father O dead on the sacristy floor, his throat slashed, a small cross etched on his chest.

Doug was hungry when he finally got home, so she warmed up leftover spaghetti and tossed together a salad for him. After he had eaten, they sat out on the porch, bundled against the chill, looking out into the dark-shrouded yard and fields beyond.

"We were five rows from the top and so far out, we were actually beyond the right field fence," Doug said. "We saw Sammy charge out right in front of us. When he hit that home run, the noise was deafening. It was like some huge beast roaring."

She reached out and patted his arm.

"I've been babbling," he said. "What's your news? Oh. Wait. I didn't tell you about parking. Did I tell you about parking? No? We were almost late, even though I left an hour earlier than I thought I had to. The traffic was just horrendous. So we parked way out on Irving—it was still thirty dollars, even that far out, if you can believe it—and started running. We forgot to turn at Clark and wound up having to double back. I'll bet we ran a mile and a half. We were both gassed by the time we got there."

He chuckled at the memory. Mo took a deep breath, gathering herself.

"And the view. We could look out and see the fans sitting on top of the apartment buildings, and beyond that, the El station, and the skyline. It was so beautiful."

"Did it make you sorry we moved?"

"No. Nice place to visit and all that."

"They made an arrest last night," Mo said. "Early this morning, in fact. He confessed to killing Father O and setting the fire at the ballpark."

"Mo, that's incredible. Who did it? It wasn't somebody local, was it?"

"No. It was that fellow who calls himself 'Weasel.'"

"The one from the chat room?"

"Yeah."

"The one you said you'd call the detective about."

"I did. I called her. She made the arrest."

He picked up his wineglass and took a sip. The glass clinked on the small table between their chairs. She caught him looking at her.

"What?"

"I have this strong feeling I'm not getting the whole story."

"I thought you didn't trust intuition."

"Where were you when they made the arrest?"

"I was... there."

"There where?"

"At his apartment."

"The murderer's apartment."

"Yeah."

"What were you doing there?"

She told him everything then. He started shaking his head long before she finished.

"In other words, you were alone with a deranged killer in his apartment, and not another living soul on earth knew you were there."

"Maurice knew."

"Who's Maurice?"

"A nice young man who lives downstairs. Everyone calls him 'Mo,' too."

Doug didn't seem too impressed to learn about Maurice.

"Doug, don't be mad. Father Mike's killer isn't roaming around loose any more."

"I understand that. I just wish you didn't have to catch every murderer yourself."

"I certainly didn't plan to. It just worked out that way."

"It's just worked out that way twice in three months."

"I'm not trying to be a detective. I swear it."

"I believe that's what you said last time."

She shrugged. He reached out, took her hand, squeezed it. "I'm just glad you're okay."

"Me, too."

He sipped his wine. "Tell me you don't wish we were a capital punishment state now. Don't you think this guy deserves to die for what he did?"

"I hope he gets the help he needs."

Doug snorted.

"Father O wouldn't want him to be put to death."

"That's true."

The phone rang inside. Mo and Doug frowned at each other. He checked his watch. "It's almost three o' clock in the morning."

"I'll get it."

He followed her into the kitchen. She snatched up the receiver. "Yes."

"Mo. Lashandra."

"What's happened?"

"He didn't do it."

"What?"

Mo sagged into the chair nearest the phone. Doug stood behind her, his hands on her shoulders.

"Weasel didn't kill the priest. We're pretty sure he did set the fire out at Mansfield Park, though."

"Why would he confess?"

"It's not all that uncommon, actually. At this point, he might even believe he did it."

"How do you know he didn't?"

"When we questioned him, he didn't know any of the details, except what was in the media. He tried to make something up."

"So, we're back to square one."

"We're back to square one. He asked me to tell you something, by the way."

"What?"

"He said he wants you to forgive him."

"Forgive him for what?"

"That's all he said. Get some sleep, huh? I'll be in touch."

"Yeah. Thanks. Good night."

"I caught the gist," Doug said when she had cradled the receiver. He circled the chair and pulled her up into his arms. He stroked her hair and kneaded the knot between her shoulder blades. "What we said still goes, though," he said. "You're through being a detective. Let's let the professionals catch the real killer."

"I promise. At this point, all I want to catch is some sleep."

"Come on, then, Scarlet. Tomorrow is another day."

†††

When Mo got up to the alarm three hours later to get ready for Mass, Doug was already out running.

She groped her way to the bathroom in a fog and ran the shower. When she stepped in, the water stung her, feeling more like an assault than the usual warming embrace.

By the time she got dressed and downstairs, it was too late to eat anything, so she settled for a glass of orange juice and a glance at the headlines of the *New York Times*.

She began to wake up—and the significance of Lashandra's phone call really sunk in—about halfway to town. If poor Bayard hadn't killed Father O, who did? As sorry as she had felt for the lonely young man who couldn't come up with a nicer name to call himself than 'Weasel,' she realized that she'd been relieved at the thought that the killer had been an outsider. It had been a shock to everyone in Mitchell when Charlie's killer turned out to be one of them. What if it turned out that way again, and Mitchell had spawned another murderer?

She went through the list of possible suspects. Frankie French, the high school teacher and would-be activist. Jacob Risley, local boy made good as a big-city developer. Juan Ortega or some other outraged member of the Tridentine congregation. Arthur Schmeiling, the outraged father. Some unknown victim of as-yet unreported priest abuse? A jilted lover? Too remote even to qualify as speculation.

And she wasn't supposed to be speculating anyway, she reminded herself as the little del Sol bottomed through the drainage ditch and into the parking lot at St. Anne's. She would try to keep her mind on praising God and seeking wisdom from His word.

But it wasn't easy.

St. Anne's was like a mission church now. Father Bakken said Mass at St. Regis in neighboring Prairie Rapids Saturdays at 5:00 p.m., stayed overnight at the rectory there, said

Mass at 7:30 Sunday morning in Mitchell, and got back to Madison in time to assist the bishop for Mass at the Cathedral.

After Mass, Mo followed the smell of coffee downstairs to the church basement, where the women's guild had prepared refreshments. She accepted a steaming cup from Hazel Rose Fenske and, God forgive her, plucked a huge chocolate donut from the tray Martha Molldrum had just set out on the counter.

"It's okay," Martha said. "We took all the calories out first."

Mo glanced toward the door just as Leona Dudley walked in, wearing a purple dress and matching hat, caught sight of Mo, turned and darted out again. Frowning, Mo took a sip of coffee, which was weak and scalding, set the styrofoam cup on a vacant table and recrossed the room. She went up the stairs and out into the parking lot.

Leona Dudley was nowhere in sight.

Granted, she'd had a rough night, but Mo was certain she hadn't imagined she'd seen the shy ex-housekeeper or that Mrs. Dudley had seemed to bolt at the sight of her.

Mo circled behind the church into the cemetery, realizing as she did that she had brought the chocolate donut with her. Something moved to her right, up the hill toward Father O's grave, and Mo turned to see a purple blur disappear behind a tree.

"Mrs. Dudley," she called out, beginning up the incline. "Leona?"

Leona Dudley stepped out from behind the tree as Mo drew near. "Hello," she said. "I didn't realize you were here."

"Are you all right?"

"Oh course I am, dear. I was just..." She looked around. "I was putting flowers on Father's grave."

Leona Dudley was carrying no flowers.

"Yes, of course." Mo could think of nothing more to say.

"Well," Leona said, looking around as if planning her escape. "I must be going. Albert will be expecting breakfast. He likes a big breakfast on Sunday."

Mo stepped aside, and Mrs. Dudley made her careful way down the slope. Mo watched her until she was out of sight behind the church, heading for the parking lot. Frowning, she trudged the rest of the way to Father O's grave, the mounded dirt still fresh and dark, the tombstone not yet in place. Someone had placed a rosary on the dirt. There were no flowers.

For a moment, Mo considered putting the chocolate donut on the grave, thought better of it, thought herself a fool for thinking it, and was halfway back down the slope when a thought froze her.

Leona had lied again, this time apparently to cover the fact that she was trying to avoid Mo. That lie somehow connected with the previous lie, the one about not having been in the rectory the night Father O was killed. Until now Mo had tried to dismiss this larger lie, attributing it to embarrassment, to an old lady's confusion, to denial that she had been so close to such a traumatic event. The thought that gentle Leona Dudley could have had anything to do with Father O's murder had seemed too monstrous to consider.

It still did. But the possibility it had been shielding now seemed so obvious to Mo, she couldn't understand why she hadn't thought of it before. What had been unthinkable now seemed a certainty.

Intuition was like that, Mo warned herself, even when it was wrong.

She hurried to her car, took the gully too fast, bottoming out as she turned onto the highway, and drove as fast as she dared through the quiet town.

Mo lost the donut somewhere, which was too bad, because a craving for chocolate surged through her.

As she turned onto the county road leading to Fireman's Park, she realized she had no plan, no idea what she was going to do. She fished her cell phone out of the glove compartment and punched in Lashandra Cooper's cell phone number.

"Hello?" a voice murmured after the fifth ring.

"Lashandra? Mo Quinn. I'm sorry to wake you."

"That's okay. I was just sleeping." Mo could almost hear the detective trying to clear out the cobwebs. "What's up?"

"I think I know who killed Father O. Can you get out here right away?"

"Wha- who?"

"Albert Dudley."

"Albert...?"

"Leona's husband."

"Why would he do that? Where are you? It sounds like you're in a car."

"I'm on my way over to the Dudleys'. Can you meet me there?"

"I'm on my way. Don't start the party without me, you hear?"

Leona Dudley's late model beige Lincoln two-door sat in the driveway of her modest little home across from the park. Mo drove past, noticing that the grass had been mowed, the low hedges lining the front of the house trimmed, the driveway sealed in preparation for winter. Storm windows were leaning against the house, waiting to replace the screens on all the windows.

Mo turned at the crossroads and came back slowly, stopping in front of a field of corn stubble next to the Dudleys' to wait for Lashandra. She felt a sudden urge to pee and regretted even the sip of coffee she'd downed in the church basement. Her stomach rumbled with hunger. The pale morning sun revealed a mass of dark clouds to the west, perhaps bringing storms. It was cold enough, she realized, for the season's first snowfall. The deer hunters would love that, as snow made tracking easier. Along with the annual "harvest" of deer, hunting season always claimed the lives of at least a handful of hunters from heart attacks, falls from tree–borne blinds, or wounds inflicted by other hunters.

She spotted Lashandra's car moving slowly up the street; relief and dread flooded her. Lashandra passed the Dudley house and pulled up next to Mo, window to window. When Mo opened her window, she noticed that the air had turned colder.

"Here's the plan," Lashandra said without preamble. "We're here to tell Mrs. Dudley that what's-his-name, Bayard, has confessed to killing Father O'Bannon. We wanted her to know right away, and we wanted to tell her in person. Does that seem plausible?"

"You want to lie to her?"

"I do not intend to lie to her. Weasel did confess. We're telling her a partial truth. We can see how she and her husband react and maybe sound out Mr. Dudley a little bit."

"Sound him out?"

"What do you want to do? Go in with guns drawn and read him his rights? We're still operating on a theory here. Not even a theory. A hunch."

"I understand."

Mo waited for Lashandra to make her U-turn and park behind her. They walked together down the street and turned in at the Dudleys' driveway. Albert stood halfway up a metal ladder, trying to pry the screen off a window at the side of the house. He gripped a long, thick screwdriver like a club, using it as a pry bar at the bottom of the screen. He wore khaki shirt and pants, clean and pressed, and a thick black belt. His work boots had been recently polished.

"Hello?" Lashandra called out as they approached the ladder. "Mr. Dudley?"

The man scowled down at them. "You don't look like Mormon missionaries," he said, his eyes darting between them.

"I think only men get to be missionaries in the Mormon Church. I'm Lashandra Cooper. I'm a detective with the Dane County Sheriff's Department. This is..."

"I know who that is." He glanced at Mo. If he was surprised to be receiving a Sunday morning visit from a sheriff's detective, it didn't register on his narrow face.

"Is your wife home, Mr. Dudley?"

"Where else would she be?"

"We'd like to talk to her."

"What about?"

"We have some news about Father O'Bannon."

"He's still dead, ain't he?" Grinning at his own joke, Albert put the screwdriver on the top rung of the ladder and stepped down.

"She's inside doing the breakfast dishes." He folded his arms across his chest and waited, his eyes moving back and forth between them.

"Thank you." Lashandra turned and went up the walkway toward the front door. Mo followed. She heard the ladder creak behind her as Albert apparently went back to his work.

Lashandra opened the screen door and rapped on the front door. Through the small window in the door, Mo could see the living room, with the pictures covering every available surface and much of the facing wall. Lashandra

234 · Marshall Cook

tried the doorbell. It emitted a stale bleat somewhere in the back of the little house.

Leona Dudley appeared in the kitchen doorway, her face clouded with concern and confusion. She hesitated, then crossed the room quickly. The door opened an inch. Mrs. Dudley peered out.

"Yes?"

"Hello," Mo said. "May we come in for a moment? We have news."

Leona Dudley's eyes flitted from Mo to Lashandra.

"This is Detective Cooper," Mo said. "Remember? You talked to her at the rectory the day ... that day."

"Nice to see you, Mrs. Dudley," Lashandra said.

"We've just had our breakfast," Leona said.

"This will only take a moment. It's about Father O'Bannon's death."

Mrs. Dudley stepped back. The door swung open. Mo stepped in, followed by Lashandra.

"I haven't had a chance to clean yet," Leona said, waving at some imagined mess behind her.

"You have a lovely home, Mrs. Dudley," Lashandra said.

"Thank you. Won't you sit down?"

"Of course."

Mo thought she heard a door click shut at the back of the house. She strained to hear more, then wondered if she'd imagined the sound.

"Would you like coffee? I baked Mr. Dudley fresh kringle. Would you like some?"

"No, thank you," Lashandra said. "We don't want to interrupt your Sunday morning any more than we already have."

"You said you had news?"

Lashandra and Mo sank onto the couch. Leona sat in the armchair across the room.

"Last night a young man confessed to killing Father O'Bannon," Lashandra said.

Leona covered her mouth with her fingers, and her eyes got very large. She looked to Mo, as if for confirmation.

Albert Dudley appeared at the kitchen doorway. "Is that a fact?" he said. "They caught him, huh? Some hoodlum kid hopped up on drugs, I bet. Didn't I tell you?" This directed at his wife. Then, to Detective Cooper, "Who was it, the Arvin kid?"

"He lives in Madison," Lashandra said. "He's a very confused young man. And he tells a very confusing story. Actually, I was hoping Mrs. Dudley could clear up a few things for me about that night. Tie up a few loose ends."

"She don't know nothing about it," Albert Dudley said. "She wasn't there." He rubbed his forehead, and Mo noticed that he had disproportionately large hands, with long, spindly fingers. "I don't know nothing about it either."

"Albert was away," Mrs. Dudley said. "Up north hunting."

"Shut up," Albert said without looking at her. "I was working the cranberry harvest. Hunting season don't start for another two weeks."

"But you said he was at home," Mo said to Leona. "Remember? You called to see if he could give you a ride home."

"She don't know what she's talking about." Albert tapped the side of his head with his right index finger. "She's getting batty. Battier."

"Where exactly were you working?" Lashandra asked, pulling out her notepad.

"Tobin's cranberry bogs. Outside Warren. You can check with them."

"I will. Thank you."

"That's up by Tomah," Leona said, drawing a glare from her husband.

"Gerry Tobin. I work for him every harvest. Been doing it for seventeen years."

"And he'll confirm that you stayed there the whole time. Is that right?"

Albert Dudley locked eyes with Lashandra, then looked away. A thick vein pulsed in his right temple. "I thought you said you caught the punk who did it."

"We're just tying up loose ends, Mr. Dudley. Trying to account for a couple of inconsistencies. You didn't come back down here during the harvest for any reason?"

"Why would I do that?"

Lashandra shrugged. "Maybe you missed your wife."

"Ha!" It was more bark than laugh.

Monona glanced at Leona. She had folded her arms across her chest and bent forward, rocking slightly, her eyes shut. "Mrs. Dudley? Are you alright?" she said.

Albert took a step into the living room. "What have you been telling them, Leona?"

"Nothing! I didn't tell them anything!"

"That's true, Mr. Dudley," Lashandra said. "She lied for you."

"I didn't do nothing. I was up north."

"And if I check the print on those boots you're wearing against the prints we found at the school after Father O'Bannon was murdered, they won't match. Is that right?"

Albert Dudley looked from Lashandra to his wife, who continued to rock in the chair, her head down, her shoulders shaking with silent sobs.

"Here's what I think happened, Mr. Dudley," Lashandra said. "I think you came back to Mitchell the night Father O'Bannon was murdered. When you got home, you discovered your wife wasn't here. You went to the rectory and found that she was staying there while you were away. Isn't that right?"

A sob broke loose from deep inside Leona Dudley.

"Shut up!" Albert lunged toward his wife.

Lashandra and Mo both leapt from the couch. Lashandra grabbed one arm, Mo the other, and Lashandra twisted Albert's left arm behind his back, bringing it up swiftly.

"Jesus! You're breaking it!"

"Quiet down, Mr. Dudley," Lashandra said. "It's all over."

Mo released his other arm, went to Mrs. Dudley, and knelt beside the chair.

Leona Dudley sobbed, her face buried in her hands. "Please forgive him," she said. "Please forgive him."

†††

Late that afternoon Mo sat with Doug on the couch in the living room sipping wine in front of the fireplace.

"So, it was basically a matter of a jealous husband," he said.

"Jealous. Possessive. Deranged."

"Father O'Bannon hardly seemed the home-wrecker type to me."

"He wasn't. He never would have violated his vows."

"I can't imagine anybody violating their vows for Leona Dudley."

"Doug. The infidelity was certainly all in Albert Dudley's head."

They sat in silence for awhile.

"I thought the meek were supposed to inherit the earth," he said. "From what I can see, the vicious and the rapacious seem to have a pretty good lock on it just now."

When she didn't respond, he put his arm around her,

drew her close, and they enjoyed the fire in silence for a bit longer.

"You ready for a refill?" he said.

"Half a splash. I'll start getting dinner ready soon."

"I'll cook if you'd like."

"No. I'd like to make Sunday dinner."

When Doug went into the kitchen, she stood and walked over to the new bookshelves. She took down one of Father O'Bannon's first editions, *The Human Comedy*, by William Saroyan, and leafed through it.

"He called these his thorn in the flesh," she said when Doug came back in.

"What are you going to do with them?"

"Keep them. Read them."

"I thought you'd already read them."

"Some of them. They can bear re-reading."

"I guess there are a few here that I could benefit from reading. If that's okay."

"Of course it's okay."

"Maybe I'll start with this one." He pulled down William Faulkner's *The Sound and the Fury*.

"That one should carry a warning label. It's pretty tough going."

"For a financial analyst, you mean."

"For a human being, I mean. I've read it twice and still don't know what's going on for long stretches."

"Then why do you read it?"

"It moves me." She smiled at him. "Same as you. I don't understand you, but you move me."

He bent down and kissed her. "Me and Willie Faulkner, huh?"

"It's not quite the same thing."

"Glad to hear it. Let me get dinner started. You just sit and relax."

"You sure?"

"Yes. I'm sure."

When he left, she sat in one of the armchairs and examined the Saroyan. In the cover illustration, a smiling little boy in overalls was waving to a black man, who was waving back from the freight train he was riding.

A small slip of lined notepaper marked a place in the book. She opened to that page and read the note, recognizing Father O's writing.

We live in the dark.
We do the best we can.
The rest is the madness of art.
—Henry James

She started reading from the page that had been marked.

"Only good men weep. If a man has not wept at the world's pain, he is less than the dirt he walks upon because dirt will nourish seed, root, stalk, leaf and flower, but the spirit of a man without pity is barren and will bring forth nothing."

She cried and couldn't read anymore. She slipped the note with the Henry James quotation back in the book and closed it. For awhile she just sat, listening to Doug working in the kitchen.

She stood and put the book carefully, lovingly back on the shelf and went into the kitchen to help with dinner.

MARSHALL COOK is most recently the author of the novel *Murder Over Easy*, the non-fiction book *The Great Wisconsin Manhunt of 1961*, and over 20 other books on baseball, creative writing and time managment. His book *Slow Down and Get More Done* landed him an appearance on the Oprah Winfrey show. Born in Altadena, California, he now resides in Madison, Wisconsin with his wife Ellen where he is a popular professor of creative writing in the University of Wisconsin-Madison Division of Continuing Studies. He is the editor of *Creativity Connection*, a newsletter for writers.

Made in the USA
Middletown, DE
16 September 2023

38616550R00146